THE DARKNESS AT WINDON MANOR

Frederick Faust
(Max Brand)

The Apes of Devil's Island

BY JOHN CUNNINGHAM

The Exploits of Beau Quicksilver

BY FLORENCE M. PETTEE

The Flying Legion

BY GEORGE ALLAN ENGLAND

The Golden Cat:
The Adventures of Peter the Brazen, Volume 3

BY LORING BRENT

The Opposing Venus: The Complete Cabalistic Cases
of Semi Dual, the Occult Detector

BY J.U. GIESY AND JUNIUS B. SMITH

The Radio Menace

BY RALPH MILNE FARLEY

The Ruby of Suratan Singh: The Adventures
of Scarlet and Bradshaw, Volume 2

BY THEODORE ROSCOE

The Sheriff of Tonto Town:
The Complete Tales of Sheriff Henry, Volume 2

BY W.C. TUTTLE

The Vengeance of the Wah Fu Tong:
The Complete Cases of Jigger Masters, Volume 1

BY ANTHONY M. RUD

THE DARKNESS AT WINDON MANOR

MAX BRAND

INTRODUCTION BY

WILLIAM F. NOLAN

ALTUS PRESS
2018

PUBLISHING HISTORY

"Introduction" appears here for the first time. Copyright © 2018 William F. Nolan. All rights reserved.

"The Darkness at Windon Manor" originally appeared in the April 21, 28, May 5, and 12, 1923 issues of *Argosy* magazine (Vol. 150, No. 6–Vol. 151, No. 3). Copyright © 1923 by The Frank A. Munsey Company. Copyright renewed © 1950 and assigned to the Frederick Faust Trust. All rights reserved. Images copyright © 1923 by The Frank A. Munsey Company. Copyright renewed © 1950 and assigned to Steeger Properties, LLC. All rights reserved.

"About the Author" originally appeared in the December 10, 1932 issue of *Argosy* magazine (Vol. 234, No. 5). Copyright © 1932 by The Frank A. Munsey Company. Copyright renewed © 1960 and assigned to Steeger Properties, LLC. All rights reserved.

THANKS TO

Everard P. Digges LaTouche, Richard Mann, and William F. Nolan

Visit *altuspress.com* for more books like this.

TABLE OF CONTENTS

WILLIAM F. NOLAN

HERE IS A clever, charming, old-fashioned crime tale. Not old-fashioned for the period (1923) but a far cry from the tough-guy school as developed by Dashiell Hammett in the pulp pages of *Black Mask*. Frederick Faust (better known by his primary pen name, Max Brand) would later write much harder-edged novels in the Hammett tradition ("The Dark Peril," "Cross Over Nine") but "The Darkness at Windon Manor" is definitely "old school." Criminals are presented here as gentlemen; there is much bowing and formal talk. Written when overseas travel was common, the story begins with an odd conversation aboard an ocean liner bound for America. (Such a trip was familiar to Faust, who often booked passage from his home in Europe to confer with editors in New York.)

"The Darkness at Windon Manor" features his oft-used theme of mistaken identity ("Montana Rides!," etc.). However, it is presented here with a unique twist. Andrew Creel, Faust's protagonist, finds himself identified as a key figure in the dark world of high crime. Faust is full of surprises. The story's female lead, beautiful Anne Berwick, proves to be a jewel thief, and Creel finds himself drawn to her and to a life of crime like a drug he cannot resist. It is as if Creel is two men in one. How he handles this perplexing situation forms an off-beat tale that offers intrigue and romance in equal measure.

A missing case of precious stones, a wildly dangerous automobile ride, and a bold daylight bank robbery all add to the action.

"The Darkness at Windon Manor" is sheer pulp melodrama. You may not believe it, but you won't forget it.

Prolific award-winning author William F. Nolan (best known for Logan's Run*) is the leading global authority on the life and career of the legendary Frederick Faust ("Max Brand"). Celebrated as "The King of the Pulps," creator of Dr. Kildare, and (among 250 Western novels)* Destry Rides Again, *Faust was killed in action in 1944 while serving as a war correspondent during the Italian Offensive in World War II. (Kildare was named after county Kildare in Ireland—and Faust had used the name earlier for his pirate hero Ivor Kildare.)*

William Nolan has edited six books on Faust: three volumes of his best Western stories, two collections of classic Faust tales, and a book of his best crime stories. His pioneering volume, Max Brand: Western Giant *(1985) lists all of Faust's 25 million words of fiction, his plays, non-fiction, verse, films (adapted from his works), radio, stage, and TV productions, and compiles memoirs and essays relating to Faust's life and career.*

Since the 1950s Nolan has written extensively about Faust (and his 20 pen names) for a wide variety of markets. He has seen his work appear in each issue of Singing Guns, *a magazine devoted to Faust, and in* The Max Brand Companion. *For many years he was a close friend of Faust's eldest daughter, Jane Faust Easton, and her husband, writer Robert Easton, now both deceased. Nolan's novel,* Rio Renegades, *is an homage to Faust. Also, working with the Eastons, he compiled* Max Brand's Best Poems *in 1992.*

Nolan's collection of works by and about "Max Brand" includes 1,100 books and nearly 600 full-issue pulps, and remains the world's largest.

CHAPTER I

THE SENSE OF LOSS

THOUGH THE CHAIR in which he sat was one of a long and closely filled line, Andrew Creel seemed sufficiently aloof. It was not that the steamer rug wrapped closely about his knees or the cap drawn far over his eyes differed from those of the men near him, not that his lean face and dark eye were forbidding in any degree; but he carried about him that air of self-completeness which does not invite inquiry.

Conversation, after all, generally starts with discomfort of mind or body. When a man is lonely, or too hot, or too cold, or wearied of his surroundings, he turns to a neighbor who seems to suffer mutually; he voices a common protest, and the conversation begins on common grounds. It is not hard to tell when a man is ready for and open to approaches. A slight wandering of the eye, a yawn which never springs from sleepiness, a sullen drooping of the mouth, a nervousness of hand and foot—these are the signs which betray a man who pines for conversation.

But Andrew Creel was one of those who can be heated neither by conversation nor wine, nor by a tropic sun; they cannot be crowded in a throng, and they cannot be made lonely in a desert. They neither criticize nor protest nor praise. They merely watch; and one cannot tell whether their observations are retained in mental notes or consigned to oblivion. All down the line of steamer chairs there were perpetual changes. Some one leaned forward to draw his rug closer or loosen it; some one rearranged his hat; some one leaned back and tried to sleep

1

with a scowl on his forehead, as if defying any one to accuse him of ill success; but Andrew Creel seemed utterly unmoved. His hands never altered their position in his lap; a corner of his rug had worked loose in the wind, and it flapped unheeded; his head turned from time to time, slowly, never jerked about by irritation or curiosity.

Indeed, it seemed as if the quiet eye of Andrew Creel found something new in each one of the vast groundswells which heaved about the side of the ship and went wandering off against the distant sky line with ridges of white and little rushings of foam along its sides. The swagger of the ship on the crest of the wave and its drunken lunge into the hollow of the trough seemed equally soothing to him. When people passed, the eye of Creel followed them calmly down the deck at times, never prying and never omitting the slightest detail.

It did not irritate those he observed, for they knew that he noted, but felt that he made no criticism; it was not much more than the observant eye of an animal. Again, he fairly looked through a whole group and bent his observation past them on the familiar rise and fall of the waves. One could never prophesy his state of mind; he might be on the verge of whistling a tune or closing his eyes in dreamless sleep.

In fact, Creel was very much what he seemed. He had spent a number of years wandering the earth, living well within the limits of a comfortable income. In all places he was at home, and he became the back of a camel in Egypt as well as the saddle on a spirited horse in Central Park. Bohemia accepted him in Paris without a murmur, and respectability opened its doors to him in London. What he gained from his wanderings no one would be prepared to guess, for he had never opened his heart to a confidant. It was really hard to conceive of such a man having a confidant. And though one presumed that under stimulation he might be a most fascinating narrator, it was obvious that nature intended him for a listener rather than a talker.

Life had left him as unmarked within as his forehead was smooth without. He was a man untested, untried. If there was strength in him, it was like the speed of the pedigreed horse which has never trodden a race track. He did not make an appeal vital enough to stimulate wonder and puzzling estimates; perhaps he might have been called the Sphinx without her smile. At the most, people surmised in him cleanness of body, heart and mind; and probably Andrew Creel made no more definite estimate than this of himself. He had no enemies, and yet he did not feel ineffectual; he had no friends, and yet he was never lonely.

On a gray day he mildly enjoyed the dimness; on a bright day he mildly enjoyed the color. He did not object to liquor, and yet he had never been drunk; he found women amusing, but he had never been in love; he enjoyed money, but he never yearned hungrily for silken luxury. To be sure, he was not asleep, but one could not help asking: "What if this man should awaken? What if he should desire, dread, hate, love? What if the black and white of his life should be flushed with sudden color—golden, reds, and purples?"

This very question in much the same words passed through the mind of Creel as he sat in the sunshine of the deck of the steamer. The stimulus to the question was a man who stood half facing him at the rail. This fellow had taken his hat off and the sea breeze was ruffling his hair; his head was bent a little back, and with partially closed eyes and faintly smiling lips he breathed deep of the same wind. Undoubtedly, Andrew Creel had seen a hundred other men in similar postures and had never been stirred to question or to comparison of their mood with his own. The difference this time lay in the similarity which existed between the bareheaded man and himself.

Not that they at all approached the same identity. To be sure, no one could ever mistake them; but they belonged to the same physical type. There was the high, rather narrow forehead, with marked prominences just above the eyebrows, the straight lips, the thin chin, the arched nose, the dark, sallow complexion, the black eyes, the lean, erect body suggesting agility rather than downright strength, endurance rather than sudden bursts of speed.

It was the call of like to like which first drew Creel's sharp attention. He noted one by one with unerring eyes the similarities, and in the second place he enumerated the differences. Here, however, there were difficulties. No matter how he concentrated on the subject, he could not make a list of the distinctions. His strong sense of order revolted against this failure. It was finally borne in upon him that the distinction was mostly a matter of differing spirits.

This man had rubbed shoulders with the world, had trodden the race track of human competition. The parallel lines had been engraved between his eyes by strife, victory, and perhaps defeat. He was capable of sorrow; he was capable of joy. Ah, there was the vital thing!

The salt wind in the face of Creel, which was a mere physical fact, made the stranger straighten his body and close his eyes in exquisite enjoyment. Creel caught the sense of the other covering space; that wind blew him into the past—how far? and into the future—how far? What keen associations pierced with that wind into the center of his being? For the first time in his entire life Creel was conscious of a hollow sense of loss, of desire. He had missed something in life. What was it?

The questions we ask ourselves cannot be evaded. Andrew Creel discovered with infinite discomfort that he could not turn his shoulder on himself as he had turned his shoulder on the world. He made, at last, a silent, sharp resolution to pierce the secret of this other man; to seek him out; to open him like a book and read therein. That resolution was the turning point in his life. He felt like the man who sits half dozing by the fire until a sudden thought comes knocking at his mind and he startles erect with the feeling that some one else has been in the room and watching him. Indeed, considering Creel in the light of what he did thereafter, it might be said that he had never before been awake.

CHAPTER II

THE DESTROYER

UNACCUSTOMED AS CREEL was to feel under the positive necessity of meeting any human being, he was in doubt as to how he should approach the stranger. It seemed clumsy to go to him with some direct question in front of the crowd of languid passengers. He stared down, concentrating on the problem, and when he looked up again the stranger was gone.

He noted it with a quickening of the heart. There was no doubt now that he *must* exchange words with this man. Eventually he sauntered around the deck, but the stranger was nowhere in sight, and Creel carried his disappointment down to dinner with him. His gloom was the greater because this was the last evening on board ship, and the next morning everybody's time would be taken in the bustle of making port: in fact, by sunrise they would be among the approaches to New York. To-night was his last chance to find his man.

After dinner, accordingly, he went directly up to the deck. Once there, it was the wind which led him, for it was strongly connected in his mind with his earliest picture of the other. Creel went straight forward to the point where the wind was sure to be strongest—the bow. He was correct. There, leaning on the railing and apparently watching the bow wave, was his quarry. So sharpened were his eyes for the search that he recognized his man by the shape of his back.

Creel approached slowly, pondering ways of opening the conversation, when the wind which had already helped him assisted him again. It flipped the hat from the head of the other and whisked it straight into the hands of Creel. He laughed; there was exultation in his voice, for he knew that chance was playing into his hand.

"The Lord be praised," said the stranger, "for you've saved the only thing about me that won't be alien in America." He touched the hat into shape, for the crown had been deeply indented, and replaced it on his head.

"You see," he explained, "before I left London I intended to get clothes from an American tailor—a whole outfit—but I dodged the job until the last moment, and then I only had time to get a hat."

"Well," nodded Creel, as he took a position at the rail near the other, "we're certainly exact opposites; the only thing American about you is your hat, and the only thing English about me is the same article. Yet on the whole I prefer English styles throughout."

The other shrugged his shoulders. He said:

"We're on the way toward making comparisons between the English and Americans. Let's avoid it."

"And why?" asked Creel. "To the end of the world we'll remain interested in our differences; I've never known an American who could spend an hour in London without making comparisons between it and New York, and *vice versa*. There are very good reasons for it."

"Aye," replied the other, "cousins are always curious concerning each other."

"Exactly. We're just enough alike to make us appreciate our differences."

"And just close enough to fail to see each other in perspective."

"To be sure," agreed Creel. "We forget that we speak the same language, and remember that we have differing accents; we habitually underrate each other, and yet, when it comes to a pinch, blood usually tells. Still, the habit is irritating."

"Good again. The Yankee calls the Englishman dull, and the Englishman calls the Yankee cheap."

"But give them both the same environment, and you can't tell them apart, perhaps, in a single generation."

"To be sure; we have the same thieving ancestry," said the stranger.

"Thieving?" echoed Creel.

"Well, why not call it that?" argued his companion. "What other is the ancestry of the Englishman and the American? Not that I mean that we are still thieves, but we gained our strength from a strong infusion of the bloods of predatory races. In the beginning the Celts were in Great Britain. They were harmless enough to the world; they injured no one but themselves. At the same time they accomplished no particular good; they added nothing to the civilization of the world. They're a comparatively new race, and yet they left so few monuments and influences that they're almost prehistoric. They didn't try to take from others, but neither did they give to others. But then came the robber Saxons. They were an element of aggression and strength. They made a mark.

"Next came the robber Danes. Another element of strength. Finally came the robber Normans. Four elements of blood go to the making of the modern Englishman—and American— and three of those elements are from predatory races. They all had the acquisitive impulse, so that they stole at first, and when there was nothing else to steal they began to make for themselves."

He broke off and chuckled to himself, then he added, nodding in self-agreement: "Yes, we call the Englishman's instinct to conquer and rule to-day imperialistic instinct, but I wonder if it isn't a lineal inheritance from the spirit of the Vikings."

"Ah," murmured Creel, "you believe that the thief and the creator are only short steps apart?"

The other started and turned more directly toward Creel. His eyes sharpened.

"In a manner of speaking," he said, "that's exactly what I *do* mean. Come, come! We begin to agree famously!"

"Well," answered Creel, "it's a new viewpoint, but I suppose a fairly sound one. The impulse of the thief is to have and to hold; so he takes what some one else has already made. But if there's nothing to take he makes it for himself. He raises his own grain, perhaps."

"Or irrigates the desert," added the other.

"Or paints his own picture."

"Quite right. One generation steals a country to which their only title deed is the stronger hand; the next generation cele-brates the theft with an epic poem. Superior strength, superior subtlety makes the theft possible; and strength and cleverness are the materials which the poet wants for his singing, his idealization."

"According to this," said Creel, smiling, "the thief is a very important and necessary element in civilization."

"And why not admit it?" answered the other with a touch of sharpness. "Strength is the important thing in men, and thieves are strong. They pit their single power against the banded might of the law. The primitive impulse which the average man reduces to spite, jealousy, backbiting, the thief admits to himself and follows. At least, he is not a hypocrite, and hypocrisy is the damning sin of every other class of society."

"Now we have reduced it to this," summed up Creel: "the thief is strong, clever—and honest." He laughed softly.

"You laugh," nodded the other, "but nevertheless you agree with me!"

And in spite of the growing dimness of the evening Creel saw that his eyes lighted with triumph. He added:

"Paris stole Helen: hence Odysseus and Agamemnon and Achilles; hence Homer. It all began with a theft; and after all, when does a good man make a satisfactory hero? He may be impressive, but he can never be real.

"The hero of Paradise Lost, every one admits, is Satan. Our

sympathies lie with Abel; our interests lie with Cain. The destroyer holds the center of the stage. Caesar stole their rights from the populace; and the populace dropped upon their collective knees and thanked him for it. Yes," he concluded, "for a life which gives a man excitement, pleasure, leisure, and a light conscience, give me the profession of the thief."

As he ended, a searchlight from the bridge, whose shaft of light had been wandering wildly across the clouds, now dropped for an instant toward the prow of the ship and fell upon the figure of Creel's companion. His hand flew up automatically, as if to ward a blow. In raising it the two middle fingers were closed, but the forefinger and the little finger remained extended stiffly. It was an odd gesture; even when the searchlight flashed away the oddity of it remained imprinted on the mind of Creel. For no real reason he wished suddenly to be alone; to think over and analyze at leisure the host of impressions which the stranger had given him.

"I have to get my things in shape for the landing," he said, "so I'll bid you a very good evening. And perhaps," he added, "we can meet again in the morning? Perhaps we can find other points for agreement, eh?"

"By all means," chuckled the other, "and suppose we make this the meeting place—any time after breakfast. I'm usually out here watching the gallop of the bow wave and catching the breath of the wind. The wind, my friend—there's the predatory spirit for you!"

It was full night as Creel turned away and walked back up the deck. He remembered, after he had gone a little distance, that he had forgotten to ask the name of his new found friend, and he turned sharply about. He was loath, however, to return for such a purpose; it was too blunt, too crass a question; it showed too much curiosity, and if there was one thing on which Creel prided himself, it was his profound indifference.

As he stood, hesitating, he saw a broad-shouldered, stocky man walk down the deck toward the prow. The eye of Creel followed him, partly because of his powerful proportions, partly because his head was canted in an odd, thoughtful manner to one side, partly because he was walking straight toward the place where the stranger stood at the prow watching the rushing of the bow wave, faintly white, below. But the night was now so thick that the eye of Creel did not reach to the prow itself. Into that gloom the figure of the stocky man with the canted head disappeared. At that Creel turned and went slowly to his cabin.

CHAPTER III

THE SIGN OF ORMONDE

THE NEXT MORNING breakfast was hardly done when Andrew Creel went straight to the bow. It was already crowded with passengers who kept their eyes fixed on the approaches to New York Harbor, and among them there was no sign of the interesting stranger of the night before. It irritated Creel but hardly surprised him, for the stranger was distinctly not the man on whom engagements lie heavily; he would follow his mood.

Creel waited patiently, and when his man did not appear he made a careful tour of the decks. He regretted doubly now that he had not learned the name of his singular acquaintance, but finally he resigned himself to his fate. They were already in the heart of the harbor—the jagged outline of the Battery was like a row of lances cutting into the sky.

It was not hard to dismiss the stranger, no matter how promising their talk had been, for it seemed to Andrew Creel that he had already caught at the secret. The feeling that he had slept all his life was stronger than ever in him; it made the consciousness of his present alertness all the more keen. He fell to watching the faces of men and women and children who passed him. To be sure, this had always been a favorite amusement of his, but there was now a difference.

Whereas he had formerly merely caught at the characteristics and type of a man, he now tried to go back into his past, and from that he tried to build the man's future. It seemed to

Creel in the delight of his new attitude that every line in a man's face was as significant as a chapter in a biography. Aye, every man was an open book, though each was written in a differing language; but everything helped Creel—the shape and activity of hands, the set of a chin, the brightness of an eye, the carriage of head and shoulders.

Not men alone, but the very feel of sun and air was new to Creel, and the distant heights of the Battery were like a jumble of imperial towers over a fairy city; when he stepped ashore he would be in the land of adventure. It was strange that a glance at a man and five minutes conversation should have affected him so vitally, but perhaps Creel had merely reached the natural end of his period of inertness.

After all, most men reach some such awakening. To some it comes through the sudden love for a woman, disappointed or fulfilled. A lesser thing affected it with Creel; he was as changed from himself of yesterday as the adolescent is removed from the mature man. It was not strange, therefore, that he was whistling as he moved down the gangplank, and when at last he was free to pass on into the city he walked with a springing, eager step like an athlete from whose shoulders a weight had been removed.

It was as he passed in the steady stream of people out onto the street that a form of great height loomed suddenly at his elbow, and a voice boomed:

"Hel-*lo!*"

He whirled, shaken with surprise, and his hand automatically flew up as if in self-defense; but when it rose the middle fingers were clenched and the fore and little fingers stiffly extended in the manner of the stranger on the ship the night before. He dropped his hand at once and found himself looking up into the face of a burly monster a whole head taller than himself; a man with a comfortably rounded vest and a plump face, tinged with the pink of good living. His eyebrows were so highly arched and his eyes so wide and extraordinarily blue that his expression was one of the most extreme candor and naïveté.

Before the gesture of Creel he started, and the color in his face deepened; his eyes darted once to right and left, and brushing close to Creel he muttered:

"Good God, Ormonde, do you give that sign in public places?"

The blood leaped from the heart of Creel to his head and then back again. He stared straight before him; the sun had never been so bright—faces were a swirl of dazzling white in that radiance. For the dream of the morning was true: he had stepped into a land of adventure—a fairyland. Ormonde? Well, he would be Ormonde or any one else for the nonce. The words came of themselves; his volition had nothing to do with them. He said:

"My dear fellow, it's become a second nature to me, and there's really no danger in it."

And to prove it he brazenly raised his hand in the same manner with the two fingers stiffly extended. The big man cursed softly; he was so excited that his forehead gleamed with sweat.

"Damnation, Ormonde!" he muttered. "Are you going to turn out as bad as everything we've heard about you? Follow me—this way!"

He led the way to an automobile, a long-bodied roadster, and they began to wind away through the heavy traffic with horns blaring about them and the rumble of trucks over the cobblestones.

"You took me on trust from the signal?" cried the giant in a voice that boomed easily over the rush of traffic.

"Not altogether," smiled Creel.

"Ah, I suppose that Anne said a word about me?"

"More than a word, in fact," replied Creel. "Quite a lengthy description."

"H-m!" rumbled the other, and his pink face turned red with

pleasure. "A damned good girl—Anne! Did she call me Uncle Larry or just plain Payson?"

There was a note of concern in his question.

"Uncle Larry," replied Andrew Creel.

"Good!" nodded Payson. "She and I are as thick as—ha! I always choke over that word, Ormonde, damn it!"

"Naturally," said Creel.

"Eh? Naturally."

The big man swung about in his seat to stare at his companion in such amazement that he avoided a passing street car by the least portion of an inch. But Creel leaned back against the cushions perfectly at ease. He had never been more pleasantly stirred in his life, and he was inwardly sworn to see this adventure through.

"Tut, tut!" he protested. "Are you about to quarrel over a word?" And then he made his first wild venture toward the truth.

"Can't I step out of the profession for a single instant?"

"To be sure! To be sure!" agreed the other. "You are talking unofficially, so to speak. That's a good one!" He laughed thunderously. "But I'm not going to quarrel about the word. No, Ormonde, I'm a little too conservative to quarrel with you."

He laughed again, but this time without much mirth. "You see, we have heard a little of your history."

"I hope," murmured Creel, "that you enjoyed it."

"Enjoyed?" echoed Uncle Larry Payson. "By the Lord, Ormonde, I tell you my hair stood on end during part of it, particularly that whole Marborough episode. D'you know that when I heard how they both arrived at the same time I gave you up—I buried you!"

"Really?"

"You think I should have had more confidence in you than that? Well, sir, I have! After that yarn was done I was prepared to believe you could go through solids like an X-ray, and now that you have the Bigbee case—well, sir, when we get home I'll tell you at length what I think of you and what all the rest of the boys think of you. We are agreed on that. In fact, Ormonde, your fame has spread abroad through America among others than us. Yes, sir, you'll be delighted with a tribute that was paid you the other day. I was dining with the new police commissioner."

"With the police commissioner!" echoed Creel rather more than politely surprised.

Payson smiled with fatherly benevolence.

"We are thick—the best of friends," he went on. "I am one of the advisory cabinet, so to speak, and confer with the chief on his most difficult cases. He considers me a rare amateur in crime."

"An amateur?" repeated Creel, and then laughed softly. His mirth was mightily re-enforced by Payson.

"Yes, sir, those are the words of old Tom York, God bless him! An amateur in crime! If he knew the truth he would not believe what his eyes and ears told him. But I was about to tell you of the compliment he paid you. We had a good deal of wine with dinner, and Tom grew rather warm. He began to talk about big cases he knew of—in fact, he gave me some invaluable information that I'll tell you about later. In the midst of things he began to talk about the greatest criminals the law has combatted. And finally he said:

" 'There's a young fellow in England the world will hear of one of these days. I've heard of some of his exploits, but not all of them. In fact, I've reason to believe that no one dreams of half the things he has done. His name, I understand, is Edward Ormonde, and in my personal opinion, Mr. Payson, he is the greatest thief that ever lived.' How's that, Ormonde?"

Creel flushed and was silent.

"You aren't offended?" inquired Payson eagerly.

"The word won't do!" said Creel decisively. "Won't do at all, in fact. Thief? Pah!"

"To be sure," cried Payson hastily. "I don't mean to circum-scribe your talents to the one branch. By no means! And for that matter neither did Tom York, I'm sure!"

"Let it go," said Creel, relenting. "But it always irritates me a little to hear a fine—er—art, degraded with the name of thievery!"

Payson coughed and swallowed his smile, but by a mighty effort he presented a fairly straight face to Creel, though the cost was swelling purple veins above his forehead.

"If Edward Ormonde calls it an art," he said, "why, an art it is!"

CHAPTER IV

CROSSING THE RUBICON

THE LONG ROADSTER by this time was humming softly on its way across the Fifty-Ninth Street bridge. In a few minutes it had cleared the suburbs of Brooklyn and was rushing along a country road. Since the remark about theft being an art Payson had few comments to make. Presently, however, he pointed to the left.

They had just topped a hill and they looked down upon a promontory. It was a triangle, the point touching the mainland, while the ocean surrounded it almost completely from the three sides. Down to the sea it dropped in sheer cliffs and at the bottom of these Creel saw the white lines of the surf and caught the far-off murmur of its rolling. The top of the promontory rose smoothly up toward the center, a fine lawn covering the outer portions and the mansion rising in the center, surrounded with mighty trees.

"Anne sent you a picture of it, didn't she?" went on Payson, as though irritated by the persistent silence of Creel. "Recognize it?"

"It shows even finer than it did in the picture," answered Creel. "In fact, I've rarely seen a finer place!"

"H-m!" nodded Payson. "That's what I say—though it's throwing a bouquet at myself—for I chose the site myself, you know, and I supervised the fitting up of the house. All that left wing is my work, besides the stables and the garage. We call the place Windon Manor."

"The whole group of buildings hangs well together," agreed Creel. "You did a good job of that. I suppose it's much admired."

They were sweeping down the graveled road from the crest of the hill toward the gate in the stone wall which crossed the neck of the promontory.

"The trouble is," answered Payson regretfully, "that men in our profession are usually too busy with other things to pay much attention to architecture. I can't tell you how glad I am to see that you're not like the general run. Naturally, men outside the profession never enter the grounds."

"Naturally," echoed Creel noncommittally, "you couldn't let men of another sort enter."

"I should say not," sighed Payson. "We'd venture daylight murder to keep others out."

Coming down the sweep of the hillside the car had gathered terrific momentum.

"Really?" murmured Creel. "And what would you do if a man not in your—or our—profession, got into the house or even the grounds? Would you actually go so far as murder?"

"Murder?" cried Payson. "Good Heavens, Ormonde, don't you see that it would be absolute ruin for an outsider to come in with us—even at a distance? We couldn't take a chance. There are things in that house that might—but let's not talk of the danger of an outsider getting in! It sets my blood running cold, the very thought! Murder? Why, Ormonde, we'd have to kill the unfortunate beggar and burn his body to ashes in the furnace. We'd have to annihilate him and every trace of him!"

Here the car, striking a slight rise of ground just before the gate, seemed to rise from the road and leap like a winged thing through the gate. Andrew Creel settled back against the cushions, his eyes half closed.

"But," said Payson, easing up the speed of the machine as they approached the house, "we give every one who comes here the acid test and you may be sure we know their history backward before they are trusted."

"And yet," said Creel, driven by the imp of the perverse, "just how much do you know about me?"

"Of course not much," chuckled Payson, "but then you would be an exception in any society—absolutely!"

"I wonder!" murmured Creel, and glancing back over his shoulder he noted the gate far behind him. He felt as if he had crossed the Rubicon, indeed.

They ran the car into a roomy garage, and a mechanician in a greasy cap approached them as they walked back toward the door.

"This chap is our chauffeur and chief mechanic," advised Payson, "and he's as true as steel all the way through. He's never failed us in a pinch. Better stop and have a word with him. He knows you were coming and he'd be mighty happy to have you notice him." And as the chauffeur came up, "Bud, I've been telling our friend about you. This is Ormonde."

Flannery wiped his grimy hand industriously on his overalls and then extended it with some diffidence.

"Glad to know you," he said.

"And I," said Creel, shaking hands with a heartiness that brought light into the eyes of the other, "am mightily glad to know a man who never fails in a pinch."

Flannery grinned with overmodesty.

"Oh," he replied, "I ain't so slow on the get-away. Maybe some of the flatties know me, but they got nothing on me. I broke a leg once and done my bit, but it was only a drag. And since then the dicks have never got a whiff of my trail."

The eyes of Creel wandered slightly, but he returned gallantly to the charge.

"I believe you," he said, "and it may be that we can do a bit of work together one of these days."

Flannery swelled visibly.

"You can count me in," he said, "on anything from a gat play to soaping a peter. Why, captain, I'd go along just for the sake of watchin' you work!"

Creel waved his adieu and went on with Payson. "Gat play" and "soaping a peter" and doing a "bit" and a "drag" were far beyond his comprehension. He thanked his Creator for a liberal endowment in the power of silence.

"If you could let me have a peek at the stuff," urged Payson as they approached the house, "I'd be eternally grateful. I'd feel as if I had something on the rest of the lads."

Creel hunted desperately through his mind for an answer.

"But I suppose," went on Payson, "that you want Anne to have the first look. Well, it's her right, I guess. Personally, Ormonde, I think you're getting her cheaply even at the price of the Bigbee case; for she's a jewel among women, lad, and I'd back her with my life and everything I have. But—you don't mind if I speak frankly?—considering you in the light of your past history, I'm damned if any of us can understand how you took up with such a romantic idea as this!"

It came home to Creel for the first time clearly, and the blow of understanding stunned him. In that house was a girl named Anne with whom he was supposed to be in love; as the price of her love he was bringing from England the Bigbee case, though what the Bigbee case might be he had not the slightest dream. Hitherto, he had gathered that only the arrival of the real Edward Ormonde would reveal his identity.

But Anne—the first glance from her would disclose him to the others; and then would follow that annihilation to which Payson had referred as they rushed in the car toward the gate of the place. Yet even now, after the first shock, he was not unhappy. Boundless hope filled him: the sense of approaching danger was like wine in his blood.

The door opened before them when they had climbed the broad steps leading up to the porch and a servant, perfectly groomed as the most conservative of servants, stood holding it wide. Within Creel saw a spacious hall with a lofty ceiling; within he knew the power of the gang, whatever it might be, would close around him. There was still a chance of escape, perhaps. Yet the imp of the perverse urged him on once more. He crossed the threshold with a light step which was instantly silent on the thick rug within.

The door closed with an almost imperceptible click; the final step was taken. He gave his light overcoat and his hat to the servant. Payson had already deposited his bag and now shook a warning finger at the servant.

"And, mind you, Harry," he said gravely, "no trifling with that bag or anything in it."

"Aw, listen, chief," drawled Harry, "maybe I'm a dub, but I ain't so green as to play *him* for a fall guy!"

"That'll do!" said Payson sharply.

The servant stiffened back to his former manner instantly. The difference between it and his attitude of the instant before was as great as the change from the stiffly starched shirt from the laundry and the crumpled rag which is tossed into the laundry bag.

"Yes, sir," he said. "Very good, sir."

And past his blank stare they walked into an inner room. Here three gentlemen rose at once to greet them. They looked to Andrew Creel very much as he would have expected the owner and the guests of such a mansion to appear. They were all well past middle age; they were perfectly groomed; courtesy looked from their eyes; their manner was, one and all, the manner of the man of the world. Creel had seen such men in every great cosmopolitan city. What he had heard led him to believe them a gang of unscrupulous thieves; his senses showed him in mien and manner three complete gentlemen. Payson stepped a little away from him and bowed both to him and to the others.

"Gentlemen," he said, "I have the honor of presenting to you Mr. Edward Ormonde, of England, and now, I trust, of America. Mr. Ormonde, these are my friends and yours: Mr. John Rincon, Mr. Matthew Kingston. Mr. Robert Lorrimer."

CHAPTER V

THREE GOOD MEN AND TRUE

ANDREW CREEL SURVEYED the three cultured reprobates with a passive eye. Mr. John Rincon was very little, very withered, and very red. His complexion was so violently sanguine, indeed, that one felt as if the skin were of tissue paper thinness—as if the rubbing of the fingers against it would break the delicate tissue. It gave him an appearance of extreme boyishness which made a singularly grim contrast with the frailty of age. This contrast was sharpened, made ludicrous, by a bass voice so tremendous that it filled the apartment and came booming back from the walls; when he spoke his chest labored heavily and perceptibly.

By his side stood Robert Lorrimer. He was almost as tall as Payson himself, but not a tithe of the latter's bulk. He had a bushy, white mustache and a fluff of silver hair so thin that it stood up with every touch of a draft. His baldness accentuated a truly remarkable forehead. It was divided by a sharp line in the center, like a perpetual frown, which threw into relief the two swelling lobes of that great brow. It was his habit to speak slowly, thoughtfully, in a voice so faint and husky that at times he was almost unintelligible, and he continually paused to clear his throat.

Of the three Matthew Kingston seemed by far the youngest, but he was of that plump type who resist the approach of years. For the rest, he was quite ordinary in appearance, except that his eyes continually twinkled as though he were enjoying some secret jest. He seldom spoke, even to his intimates; he was prevented by a voice so shrill and piping that it brought an instant smile to the face of an auditor.

Accordingly, while the other three shook hands and expressed the appropriate pleasure in the introduction, Matthew Kingston murmured something unheard and let his smile take the place of words. Little John Rincon immediately took possession of Creel's arm.

"Come, come!" he said in that terrific voice. "Sit over here by the window—in that chair—so!—now we have a look at you. Well, well! So this is the great Ormonde! Sir, I shall mark this day in red chalk."

"And I," said the faint voice of Robert Lorrimer, "look forward to a long chat with you—a very long one, indeed, Mr. Ormonde!"

As for Matthew Kingston, he said not a word, but he stood with his pudgy hands clasped behind him, teetering slowly back and forth from heel to toe and smiling benignly down upon Creel.

"And where's Anne?" asked Payson. "I suppose that would be more to the point with Ormonde?"

"Of course it would, and she's due directly—she and her father. A dear girl, Ormonde, and we envy you your good luck!"

So saying, he rubbed his little, clawlike hands together and laughed with deafening heartiness.

He continued: "They'll be in directly; they didn't expect to see you here so soon. Quick trip, Payson, old boy!"

"And now," suggested Robert Lorrimer, "a peek at the Bigbee case, eh?"

"Not at all!" protested Payson, and he raised his big hand. "Not at all! Let Anne have the first look at 'em. After all, she's to pay the price!"

His chuckle over this witticism called forth a soft-voiced but stern rebuke from Lorrimer:

"My dear Payson, you are not in the slums, you know. You really are not. I wish you would watch your vocabulary."

"Rot!" blurted Payson. "Ormonde's a man: he takes no offense at a harmless little jest."

"At least," murmured Lorrimer, "Mr. Ormonde is a gentleman; and as such he will forget. Well, Mr. Ormonde, we all regret that our chief is not here to welcome you; but perhaps you're already acquainted with him in some other place? His name is James Ashe—to his friends."

"I have never had the pleasure," answered Creel.

And he wondered at the man who could be named chief in such a circle of accomplished scoundrels.

"It is to be regretted," said Lorrimer. Here he lowered his voice so that there was a singular emphasis on all that followed, though it may have been due to the constitutional weakness of his throat. It gave the impression that he excluded the others in the room from his comments, as though Ormonde alone could understand and appreciate. He said:

"It's a full month since Ashe left us. In fact, he departed almost immediately after we received word of your offer, your most unusual offer, sir!"

"Unusual?" boomed Rincon. "By the Lord, yes, and most welcome! But I'd like to know this: was it for the sake of poor Berwick or for his daughter alone, or for both of them, that you have acted with this—"

"Unprecedented generosity," filled in Lorrimer. "I'll wager that both reasons operated on Mr. Ormonde—both humanity and—a love of the beautiful."

He pointed his speech with a slight and graceful bow toward Creel, who suavely replied:

"That's kind of you. And, in fact, you're right. You have described the lady yourself, and Berwick is—"

He paused, as though hunting for a word and Lorrimer, as he had expected, came again to the rescue: "A traitor," he suggested, "and a coward, but—a human being. None of us suspected him on either count until he stole the Bigbee case from us; afterwards he showed in his true colors."

"Yellow," blurted Payson, "just damned yellow—the dog!"

"Come, come!" protested Lorrimer, and he raised a thin-fingered hand. "There are qualifying remarks to make. He pretended that he wanted to make enough at a blow to retire and set up an establishment of his own for the sake of Anne. Treason? Yes, but let's bear the redeeming features in mind. On the whole, Mr. Ormonde, I'm very glad that Berwick is not to be sacrificed—though you must admit that our provocation was extreme."

"Intolerable," agreed Creel calmly. "Absolutely!"

"I'm glad you agree," sighed Lorrimer, "I wouldn't have had you think us inhuman!"

"Lorrimer!" cut in Payson. "Don't be such an infernal, cold-blooded hypocrite; don't you suppose Ormonde knows us already? Are you going to try to pull the wool over *his* eyes?"

"Payson," said Lorrimer gently, "you sadden me; you cut me to the quick!"

"Oh—" began Payson, and then shut his teeth with a click and finished his sentence by bringing a huge fist snapping home against the palm of his other hand.

"Whatever I know," said Creel, who could not refrain from smiling, "always I am glad to have my ideas amended and improved."

And he favored Lorrimer with his most courtly bow. All the time he had been measuring the four; he had been estimating their strength of body and mind. He knew that he balanced over a gulf of destruction, but the danger did not paralyze him. He recognized with a sudden wonder that he was not afraid to die. The threat suspended over his head merely served to clear his mind, sharpen his insight into the soft-voiced cruelty of Lorrimer, the brutality of Payson, the silent malice of Kingston, and the inhuman viciousness of Rincon.

What he would do he had not the slightest idea. The coming

of Anne would precipitate the final action; the coming of the real Ormonde would do the same thing.

In the little breathing space of suspense that remained to him, he found life incredibly dear, but the excitement of the moment was even more priceless.

"Thank you," Lorrimer was saying, "and, in spite of Payson, I want to assure you that it was not I but Ashe who pressed us to put Berwick out of the way; in fact, to the very end the firmness of Ashe was incredible. He was so set against accepting any ransom for the life of Berwick—even the lost Bigbee case—that I feared for a time." He completed his sentence with a marvelously expressive shrug of his shoulders.

"The truth is," broke in the thunder of Rincon, "that Ashe is pretty fond of Anne himself. He fought tooth and nail against a ransom for Berwick so long as the price of that ransom was to be Anne herself. But she settled it herself when she told him that if her father died she would lay the death at his door. Also, we voted Ashe down for the first time—even though Lorrimer was on his side!"

"Tut, tut!" said the soft-spoken Lorrimer. "Are you going to rake up old scores? It was a matter of policy, my dear Ormonde! Surely you will understand that it was a matter of mere policy; I could not consult my own humane instincts against the safety of the circle."

"Matter of mere life or death for Berwick—the cur!" said Payson. "But now you're safely here, Ormonde, I'll tell you a suspicion I've had. You see, Ashe left us immediately after we'd decided to accept your offer and spare Berwick in return for the Bigbee case. It was my personal opinion that he went to England to do you wrong—dispose of you, in fact, before you could bring the case back to us and take Anne away with you. Now I suppose Ashe merely went away to be by himself. He's terribly wrapped up in Anne, but I suppose he's submitted to the inevitable. I hope so, at least."

"Yes," roared Rincon. "A rare mind, that! He established us, you know."

"Ah," murmured Creel. "Tell me about that!"

"You do it," said Rincon to Lorrimer. "You're the orator."

CHAPTER VI

THE STORY OF A
GREAT BEGINNING

"**YOU FLATTER ME,**" smiled Lorrimer, and he went on in his slow, almost faltering manner: "You see we were all once ordinary—er—business men—all of us. Our finances were tied up in the affairs of a great bank. For obvious reasons I cannot name the bank even to you, Mr. Ormonde."

"Certainly not," agreed Creel.

"Thank you. Well, then, we were all heavily engaged to the interests of this bank, as I was saying, when it failed. Yes, sir, it failed utterly owing to embezzlement—the stupidest, most transparent embezzlement which had been going on for years, and no depositor suspected it and none of the directors.

"At any rate, the embezzling went on, and on one fine day we discovered that we were ruined—all of us. The bank couldn't pay ten cents on a dollar: a disturbance of the Street helped to tear things to pieces. Well, sir, eventually we were gathered together—twenty-two good men and true, eight years ago almost to a day. We had one common topic which bound us together—our complete financial ruin. Some one remarked that if a man of mere uninspired common sense was capable of robbing a great bank with impunity for years, a group of intelligent men would probably be able to rob the world with impunity forever. Needless to say, the man who made that remark was the very youngest of us all—James Ashe.

"In ordinary circumstances the remark would have fallen on barren ground as a mere commonplace, but we were twenty-two

29

desperate men; we felt that the world owed us some return for the honest money we had gathered and had lost."

"Honest?" growled Payson.

"As for your affairs," smiled Lorrimer imperturbably," I'm sure that I can't express a well grounded opinion."

"Well," began Payson, but stopped short, and Creel wondered to see the giant quelled by the calm voice and the smiling eye of old Lorrimer.

"We felt, I say," resumed the narrator, "that we deserved compensation and that whatever we could get, the end would justify the means. Some one took up the comment of Ashe—"

"It was yourself!" bellowed Rincon.

Lorrimer reproved him with a glance and continued:

"And supported him with a little impromptu sketch of the opportunities which might open before such an association. By the time his talk was ended others were ready to add remarks. Well, sir, that meeting lasted far into the night, though it began in the middle of the afternoon, and before the meeting broke up every member of it was pledged to secrecy and faithfulness to a new organization of a character which you may be able to surmise. We had accepted a constitution and we had named young Ashe as president. The great work was under way!"

As he paused Creel interpolated the question: "Twenty-two?"

"You naturally wonder at the number," agreed Lorrimer, "when we are now only six all told. But, you see, it was found that some of the men weakened from time to time, and the moment they weakened it was necessary that the rest of us should dispose of them. We appointed a secret committee of three to ferret out the discontented and the weak."

"And you headed the committee," commented Payson.

"And did my work thoroughly," said Lorrimer with a sudden metallic ringing of his voice, as though the memory stimulated him to an almost youthful vigor. "Did it thoroughly and would take the same steps again in case of need! When one of my committee failed me, he fell by my hand!"

His manner changed instantly, and passing his fingers through the fluff of silvery hair, he pursued his tale with a voice as soft as dripping honey:

"But those harsh days are long past, the Lord be praised! In five years the only defection has been that of poor Berwick. But to go on.

"When our number was so sorely diminished we finally decided that the remnant of the original members should no longer take an active part in the outside work except in cases of great need. We concluded that it would be wiser to constitute ourselves an inner council to plan, advise, and direct our active workers.

"These workers were recruited from various classes, beginning with what may be called the underworld of society and extending up to men of an incredibly high position. None of these was taken fully into our confidence and none was allowed to know the full extent or the details of our operations. Each was sworn, of course, to absolute secrecy, and the oath was reinforced by such proved examples of our power and instant execution of the unfaithful that our workers dread the decisions of the council far more than they dread the power of the law.

"Yes, sir, our power is felt so keenly by them that several of them have died in the chair refusing to confess to the law or to involve their directors even when pardon and police protection were offered as a reward for confession. Mr. Ormonde, I myself have witnessed two such executions, and on each occasion I was highly edified by the conduct of our unfortunate allies. They died like men; they proved themselves worthy of our society; and their names are inscribed in our memories!"

He made an impressive pause; and during it a chill went up the spine of Creel like a slowly moving piece of ice.

"As the result of these examples," said Lorrimer, "our organization is bound together with ties stronger than iron or adamant. We are dreaded more than the most horrible certainty of death; we can trust our members in every crisis. Moreover, they are forced to obey the least of instructions. They execute our orders not only in effect, but in form. In this manner we are enabled to conduct the most serious operations without unnecessary waste of life; a result which is highly gratifying to us all, needless to say!"

"Sir," said Creel, "your restraint is obvious and commendable."

Lorrimer bowed profoundly.

"Praise from Edward Ormonde," he said, "is praise indeed; but will you allow me to comment that you have not always showed the constraint which you now praise in us?"

"Explanations," said Creel carelessly, "never take much of my time. I will only say that when an end is before me I accomplish it by the most direct means. If there is opposition I destroy it; if there is revenge, I take my chance with it. And what, Mr. Lorrimer, is life without chance? It is profitable, perhaps, but very stale and weary!"

"Ah," murmured Lorrimer, "that is the opinion of a brilliant and self-confident artist, but in the end—well, each to his own preference. I prefer a longer life even if it is somewhat less crowded with action."

"And now that you've heard a little about us," boomed Rincon, "won't you favor us with something out of your own past, Ormonde? We're eating our hearts out with curiosity."

The others agreed with sparkling eyes.

"What, gentlemen, would you suggest?" asked Creel.

"The Gastonbrook affair!" cried Payson.

"The story of the two Lancasters!" said Rincon.

And the ludicrous, piping voice of Matthew Kingston now spoke for the first time: "The Van Zanten pearls!"

Creel swept them with a lingering glance of good nature.

"Ah," he said to Kingston, "I see you have an eye for the spectacular even more than the others. Now let me be perfectly frank with you: I rarely tell stories connected with my past."

He watched them exchange glances of astonishment.

"Why, Ormonde," came the roaring voice of Rincon, "we have understood that the most singular part about you is that you are always willing to confide in others any detail of your operations!"

"And so," growled the others, "have we all understood."

"No doubt, no doubt," answered Creel airily, "and as a matter of fact, that is the impression which I have always attempted to convey. But I draw a line of distinction between others I have talked to and you—my very good friends! I have talked—yes, but though I've handled the near-truth often enough, I've always avoided the exact details.

"In place of the actual happenings, when it came to the finer points, I've always substituted little touches of the imagination. For you see, gentlemen, I could not expose my methods in their entirety. I expose enough to make others believe they know all; I reserve the really distinguishing features. It is necessary. But with you, sirs, I prefer to tell the whole story or nothing at all. And of the two choices I'm sure you will forgive me if I select the second and say not a word about my past."

Lorrimer and Rincon exchanged glances, but Payson said instantly:

"That's what I call straight-from-the-shoulder talk, and I like it. Ormonde, I think more of you now than I ever have before. To tell you the truth, I've always had an idea that you were a windy, conceited, clever—damned fool. But I retract all my former opinions. And here's my hand on it!"

Before Creel could answer, Rincon announced in his terrific voice:

"And here you are, Ormonde. The lady is with us!"

CHAPTER VII

SUNSHINE

LIKE THE REST, Creel rose from his chair and turned toward the door—slowly, for when he faced that door at last he expected a sharp outcry of surprise that would bring weapons into the hands of every man in that room.

He turned, steeling his nerves, and when he saw the figure in the door he received two shocks which almost destroyed his reserve of nervous endurance. She had been riding, and she stood in the doorway, tugging off her gloves. The derby hat sat jauntily just a trifle to one side, and under it there was sunny hair, and flushed cheeks, and straight, black eyebrows. That was the singular feature—the bright hair, and the black of eyebrows and eyes.

In every respect his expectations were upset. For here was pride in place of boldness and feminine poise in place of worldly complacence. It was a darkly furnished room, high-ceilinged, of puritanically severe proportions, and spaciousness almost its only charm; she came into it like a touch of the fresh outdoors, like a sudden burst of living sunshine. At sight of Creel her eyes wavered an instant and the flush of exercise rushed into a flame of color; but at once she controlled herself and walked straight toward him, smiling faintly.

It was this that shook Creel's self-control to the core. This was the woman with whom Ormonde was supposed to be in love, and yet she did not know his face! In his utter confusion he must have betrayed himself if she had reached him, but now

34

a man came from behind her, almost trotting in haste, and rushed upon Creel.

It was a little man, plump, with a well-rounded vest that shook as he hurried forward. His face had small and regular features which had once been extremely handsome, no doubt, but good living had blurred and disfigured that face with fat, loosening the mouth, almost obscuring the eyes; and this fat, in turn, recent anxiety had converted to flabby folds.

Purple pouches were under the eyes, and grim lines ran past the mouth, and under the chin hung a loose pocket of flesh. He came now, illumined with inward light, and seized on both the hands of Creel. His own were at once cold and moist and slippery to the touch.

"You are here!" he cried when at last he could speak. "Thank God you are here at last—my boy—my son! Ormonde, God bless you for what you've done for me."

A repulsion against which he could not fight swept over Creel; he jerked his hands free and stepped back.

"I can't keep silent any longer," he said, facing Lorrimer instinctively. "I've come a long ways simply to tell you that I haven't the Bigbee case with me!"

It was singular to note the manner in which the different people received the information. Payson, the smile wiped from his face, remained staring stupidly; Rincon turned from red to purple; Matthew Kingston turned on his heel and strode toward the far end of the room; Lorrimer sat bolt upright, clasping the arms of his chair, and a devil glittered in his eyes; the girl had turned utterly white, as though one stroke of a sponge had wiped the color from her face, yet there was something akin to relief in her sigh. As for Berwick himself, he had, in spite of his repulse of the moment before, been nodding and grinning; now his nodding and his grinning continued, but his eye was blank. He turned to the girl.

"Anne," he said feebly, "what does it mean?"

Some of her color returned—a burning spot in either cheek—and her eyes fixed and narrowed upon Creel.

"I think it means what the words said," she answered slowly.

"Then God help me!" moaned Berwick, and fell rather than sank into a chair. His daughter regarded him with a singular mixture of sympathy and scorn.

"Do you expect him to help *you?*" she asked harshly, and then dropping to her knees with a little cry of sorrow, she threw her arm around his shoulder and commenced to murmur little words of comfort; the two were quite shut off from the others.

Of the rest, Creel was the least discomposed. For he had expected sudden ruin with the entrance of the girl, and now he had at least a fighting chance left him. He sat down in a chair and commenced to drum his fingers lightly on the arm.

The others remained still unchanged in their attitudes, their glances one and all fixed ominously upon him, when a whistling broke in upon them with the opening of some outer door. Lorrimer smiled without trace of mirth and turned his evil eye toward the entrance to the room and then back to Creel.

"That's the whistle of James Ashe," he said, "and he comes in good time. *He* will have something to say to you. Mr. Ormonde: and the rest of us will abide by his decision. Ah, Jimmy!"

It was a man of very broad shoulders, the rest of his body tapering down so that he gave a promise of agility as well as terrible physical strength. There was nothing distinctive about his face save the massiveness of the jaw which gave him, in repose, the expression of one who has just set his lips in determination.

"Ashe," cried Rincon in his great voice, "here's Edward Ormonde at last!"

The man with the massive shoulders started, whirled until he faced Creel directly, and then walked hastily toward him. He came to an abrupt halt half a pace away and surveyed his man with manifest insolence from head to foot.

"You!" he snarled. "You? Edward Ormonde?"

"And he came," cut in the soft voice of Lorrimer, "without the Bigbee case!"

"Ha!" said Ashe, and whirled toward the speaker. "Without the Bigbee case, did you say?"

And then, strange to say, he dropped into a chair and burst into a convulsion of laughter—homeric laughter; it seemed inextinguishable; it came roar on roar and peal on peal. It reduced him to a shaking bulk which loosely filled his chair from arm to arm. Then he sobered with an equally astonishing suddenness. He sat erect and regarded Creel with an undisguised sneer.

"So—Edward Ormonde"—and he gave the name an odd emphasis—"you came, and without the case? It was all a bluff? And just what is your purpose, my friend, in coming at all?"

"My dear fellow," said Creel, unmoved, though he understood at once that Ashe knew he was not Ormonde. "My dear fellow, in a dozen lifetimes you would never guess why I am here."

He was strong with sudden confidence; something kept Ashe from telling what he knew. Something would continue to prevent him, whatever the reason might be. On that score, at least, he was safe, until Ormonde himself appeared. But why did not Ormonde come? He was already long overdue.

"I want to call to your attention, Mr. President—" began Lorrimer coldly.

"What?" called Ashe, now grave indeed. "What do you mean by that?"

Lorrimer waved a hand of protest.

"Naturally," he said, "when Ormonde came I told him freely about our organization."

"Naturally," said Ashe with heat, "you are just clever enough to make an ass of yourself at times, Lorrimer!"

He glanced fiercely at Creel, then shrugged his shoulders and relaxed in his chair. "Well, go on."

"What I call to your attention," said Lorrimer, overlooking

the rebuke, "in that Ormonde has imposed on us, grossly. He keyed up our expectations; he led us on; he lied to us in his cablegrams."

"I only interpose to remark," said Creel, "that I have never lied to you in a cablegram."

"Ah!" said Ashe. "You never lied in a cablegram addressed to us? Well, I believe you!"

And he burst again into his heavy laughter.

"Is it a laughing matter?" bellowed Rincon, smashing his clawlike fist against his knee. "I tell you, Ashe, we've let Ormonde into our inner circle to-day! That was natural when we thought we were getting a sufficient pledge from him—and giving him one in return. But what about it now that there's no tie between him and us?"

"It's perfectly simple," said Ashe. "We remove Mr.—er— Ormonde from our midst."

"Turn him loose without any bond from him?" cried Lorrimer, "Ashe, have you departed from the last of your senses?"

"I used the word 'remove'," answered Ashe dryly, "in a sense which I was sure you, at least, Lorrimer, would not fail to understand."

"Ah!" cried Lorrimer, and a grim joy lighted his eyes. "Remove him? Good! Very good indeed. He's trifled with us and your decision is admirable—admirable!"

He sat with his glance hungrily upon Creel and his lips parted like one who drank, deeply.

"Let him be—removed—and perhaps at the same time that Berwick pays his penalty?"

CHAPTER VIII

THE FEAR OF ASHE

THIS BROUGHT BERWICK himself sharply out of his prostration. He sprang to his feet, tearing himself away from the sheltering arms of Anne, and stretched out his arms to Lorrimer.

"Bob!" he screamed. "Stand by me!"

And when Lorrimer replied with a smile so slow, so calm that he seemed to be remembering a jest from the distant past, the little man turned with a shudder to Ashe.

"Jimmy," he said hoarsely, "if I go—the way that devil Lorrimer wants—you know that you and Anne can never—"

"Stop!" cried Ashe, his face livid with restrained passion. "Berwick, you swine, do you dare to call her name in like a dirty-handed tradesman? You—"

He checked himself with infinite effort and tried to turn a calm face to the girl.

"Anne, you know I can't decide this thing by myself. You know, it's merely the will of the majority which counts?"

She answered him with a glance of scorn, and once more with the same mixture of contempt and pity she took the arm of her father.

"Don't you see?" she murmured to him. "Nothing you can say will influence them. We must leave them."

"Not this way!" screamed the little man, now hysterical with terror. "Lorrimer, I didn't mean to call you a devil! Lorrimer—Bob—old friend—you know you can save me?—you and Ashe."

His words fell away to stammering under that continual, changeless smile of Lorrimer.

"If you don't come now," said Anne fiercely, "I'll leave you to yourself!"

He shrunk instantly close to her side and clasped her arm in both his pudgy hands, saying in a broken voice:

"No, Anne! Not that! My girl, my good girl! Stand by me still. It's murder otherwise. Don't you see it? Don't you see it?"

And he went at her side from the room. Before they reached the door she was supporting almost all his staggering weight. Lorrimer turned his smile upon Creel.

"A disgraceful and unfortunate scene, Mr. Ormonde," he said, "and I apologize in the name of all the rest for it. But even in the best families—I'm sure you will understand! And now"— he glanced to Ashe—"what is to be done with our distinguished guest?"

"You have already named it," said Ashe coldly, as if the problem of Creel's disposal in no wise interested him. "But for old Berwick—the cur—I'd like to ask for a slight delay of execution."

"The good of the order before your own welfare, Ashe," cut in Lorrimer.

"I'll remember this, Bob," said the president with infinite meaning. "Remember me, too, then, and be damned!" cried big Payson. And then in a quieter voice: "Listen, Ashe. We all know how you feel about Anne, but we can't let you have her at the cost of turning Berwick loose. None of our lives would be safe for an instant. You know that if you're half the man you used to be."

The struggle which went on inside Ashe rendered him perfectly colorless and brought a gleaming sweat to his forehead. Finally he was able to say:

"The majority rules. Well, let it go at that! And I'll try to forget the bad feeling that's behind it. It remains to name the time and the means of finishing Berwick and stopping that smile."

For Creel leaned in perfect comfort against the upholstered back of his chair and surveyed the assembly with a smile that never faltered.

Here the ridiculous, piping voice of Matthew Kingston broke in: "The time—one hour from now; the means—myself!"

It suggested the cruel malevolence of a child united to the strength and purpose of a grown man, and was doubly terrible.

"Now, don't you think," came the sudden roar of John Rincon, "that Edward Ormonde is a terrific fool if he shoves his head into the noose in this fashion? Do you suppose that the man we know as Edward Ormonde would cross the Atlantic to make an ass of himself in this manner? I tell you there's something behind it!

"Even Edward Ormonde couldn't wear that smile if he didn't have something up his sleeve. Come, Ormonde, no matter what you may think now, we'll prove to you that we're reasonable and that we'll meet you halfway. What's your scheme? And if you haven't the Bigbee case, what have you done with it?"

"There's sense in that," agreed Payson. "I don't follow this game; it's too complicated for me; but I see that there's something behind the scenes."

"Why, gentlemen," answered Creel, "you honor me by suggesting that I have something up my sleeve, whether it's the Bigbee case or something else."

"Ah-h!" broke in Lorrimer. "It's clear to me! He left the case somewhere before he came out to us. He wants something more than the girl before he'll come to terms. Well, Ormonde, what the devil is it that you wish? I repeat, we're reasonable; but if you play this game too long it's liable to end with a mighty sudden period."

The face of Ashe contorted to something strangely like a smile. He said:

"I think I know the way to solve your troubles, gentlemen. But first I should like to be alone with Mr.—er—Ormonde, for a few minutes. Does any one object?"

There was general assent and the others left the room at once. Until they were gone, Ashe remained seated with his eyes fixed upon the floor; then he raised them suddenly to Creel. He was smiling openly.

"Now, sir," he said, "I saw through your bluff from the first. I haven't told the others what I know because it would have been death for you within an hour, and I admire a cool head too much to see you come to an end like that. Whatever your name is, and whatever your purpose in coming here may be, talk to me frankly, sir. If it comes to a pinch I think I can save you, but first I must know exactly who and what you are."

"I am," said Creel thoughtfully, "a pursuer of pleasure who has recently acquired a serious purpose in life."

"Very good," nodded Ashe. "An eccentric; I thought as much. Well, my friend, I'm prepared to hear you with sympathy. My own pursuits have been rather various. And now, your name?"

"Ah, there's the rub! You're sure that I'm not Edward Ormonde, it seems?"

"Come, come!" chuckled Ashe, and waved the suggestion aside.

"How sure are you?" went on Creel, for he was feeling his way with the utmost caution. He knew, now that he could secure safety if he confided everything in Ashe, but safety would be purchased at a price whose greatness he had just come to appreciate.

"I am as sure," went on the other, "as I am that my real name is not James Ashe."

"My dear fellow," smiled Creel, "that's not nearly sure enough!"

Ashe frowned.

"Besides," said Creel with unbroken calm, "you have never seen Ormonde in your life." And he added: "Face to face!"

At the beginning of that speech a faint smile touched the corners of the mouth of Ashe. At the end of it he was sitting stiffly erect and his gray eyes narrowed upon Creel.

"How do you know that?" he asked sharply.

Creel, tremendously relieved, laughed easily.

"Very well," said Ashe, "you insist on maintaining your identity as Ormonde?"

"Really," said Creel, "the name suits me as well as another. There's an aristocratic twang to it that I like, in fact."

The frown of Ashe deepened. He said: "I'm a very busy man, sir. I'm not here to trifle with you over absurdities. Come! Out with the truth! What are you?"

Creel fell back upon a touch of the mystic.

"If you knew," he said, "you would not believe the testimony of your own senses."

"You see," said Ashe, "I'm treating you with patience. I'm giving you your chance. Another question: What brought you here?"

"You already know it. Anne Berwick."

It brought Ashe to his feet.

"Anne?" he echoed.

"I knew," replied Creel, smiling up to him, "that that spur would touch you up a bit."

"I'm a very bad man to touch up," answered Ashe heavily. "A very bad man, indeed. So you came here for the sake of Anne?"

"At least," said Creel, "you may understand me better if I say that I expect to stay here for the sake of Anne."

There was a pause. At length Ashe answered in the same deep voice: "Then God have pity on your soul!"

"Thank you," nodded Creel. "I shall not need to solicit Him."

"You are either a fool or very wise or a madman," said Ashe slowly, "and I suppose you're the last of the three. But madmen, sir, are not exempted from the penalties of our order. To us you are dangerous; you know it; you persist in maintaining a silly bluff. Do I have to warn you again?

"Come! I do not dabble needlessly in blood. I assure you that the simplest thing would be for me to turn you over to the tender mercies of Matthew Kingston, but I will make one last effort to save you from your own folly. My friend, I invite you for the last time to speak openly and frankly to me!"

Creel became grave. He said:

"I know your record, Ashe. I respect it; I don't like to see you make a fool of yourself. So I will speak frankly as far as I can. In the first place, I am Edward Ormonde; in the second place I didn't come here unprotected."

"Bluff!" broke in Ashe angrily. "Childish bluff, and it doesn't work. What else?"

"Ashe," said Creel, and he rose from his chair and faced the big-shouldered man. "Look at me! Don't you see that I'm not afraid of you?"

The glance of Ashe, obediently, narrowed and pierced deep into Creel. He changed color suddenly and seemed to sway back, defensively.

"It's true," he muttered, "you're not afraid, though why in the devil you aren't is beyond me. My friend, it would be as easy for me to dispose of you as it is for me to close my hand!"

Then, for he saw that the crisis had come, Creel made the final test. He spoke in a voice as calm as before.

"I wanted to give you more time, Ashe," he said, "but if you insist on running at the stone wall, go ahead. If you're determined to bring the test of strength now—go ahead!"

He turned on his heel, for it was impossible for him to conceal his inward excitement any longer, and crossed the room to a window, his back turned squarely upon Ashe. Standing there, he slowly drew out a cigarette, lighted it, and blew a long puff of smoke toward the pane.

His heart was thundering in him; he could only pray that Ashe would not note the tremor of his hand as he raised the cigarette to his lips; and all the time he felt the eyes of Ashe burrowing into his back.

It seemed an age before Ashe said suddenly: "It's bluff, of course, but, by the Lord, it's done well enough to win!"

Here Creel turned toward him, smiling.

"I knew," he said, "that you would be reasonable."

"Well—Ormonde—" said Ashe, and he smiled in mockery as he repeated the word: "I'm going to advise my friends to give you a respite of three days. I'm going to tell them it's my belief that you have secreted the Bigbee case and that if we give you time enough you will produce it when you see that you cannot extort better terms from us. The day after to-morrow, when it is completely dark, your respite ends."

"Why," murmured Creel, "this is even more generosity than I anticipated. And what, Mr. Ashe, moves you to grant me so long a respite?"

"It's partly because I admire the coolness of your bluff," admitted Ashe, "and partly because I freely confess that you puzzle me. Nine chances out of ten, of course, there is nothing to the puzzle, but I'm going to give myself a little time to decipher you. That's all."

"All?" smiled Creel. He stepped closer to Ashe and lowered his voice while his smile persisted. "Does fear take no part in your motives, Ashe? Not a little touch of fear?"

"By God!" cried Ashe. "What are you, devil or man?"

"Fear?" repeated Creel. "At least, I hope not. It would be a blot on your very excellent record. I suggest another thing. Do you value Anne?"

The jaw of Ashe set hard, but he returned no other answer.

"Because if you do, you had better keep me away from her; give me no chance of seeing her. I warn you, Ashe."

And his smile broadened. Ashe seemed on the verge of speech, but he restrained himself like a man of deep passions, who has schooled himself to self-control.

"Because at present," went on Creel, good naturedly, "you stand much better with her than you would ever imagine, Ashe. Of course she dislikes many things about you—your violence and your frequent cruelty and a certain rough surface you have. But she admires your strength, your directness—and your love moves her. So you see, Ashe, you stand much better chances with her than you dream."

"Go ahead," said Ashe with a feeble attempt at lightness. "At least, you are amusing."

"Thank you. Keep her father from danger for a while longer; make her feel that you are his bulwark. In that way you will establish close diplomatic relations with her and who can tell what treaty might eventually be evolved!"

"But if I let her see you?" said Ashe, flushed with a growing excitement.

"Then you are lost!" said Creel solemnly. "Within twenty-four hours I will have won her completely away from you. You are right in fearing me—in two ways, Ashe."

"Bah!" snorted the big man, trembling with a strange mixture of rage and curiosity. "If I were ten years younger I might believe you. As it is, I read you like a book. Fear to let you see Anne? By God, sir, you can meet her at any time of the day or night!

I shall give directions that you are to meet her openly; I shall have her thrown together with you."

"Good again!" said Creel. "You refuse to run against the stone wall, but you are willing to jump over the precipice."

"I have other things to do now," said Ashe coldly, "and I must leave you. Remember! The day after to-morrow by the time it is completely dark, we will expect from you the surrender of the Bigbee case or something leading immediately to its recovery. Failing that—" He made a widely inclusive gesture.

"For the rest, I shall instruct that you are to have every comfort and every liberty. It is only fair to warn you, however, that your liberty has strict bounds. If you attempt to descend the cliff to the sea or if you attempt to pass beyond the stone wall which bounds the grounds, you will be instantly shot. Those limits are continually watched. I assure you, it is perfectly impossible for you to cross them alive."

"Sir," said Creel, "I have not the slightest desire to imperil my life. I will cling close to the safety of the house."

"As for that," replied Ashe, "you are the judge. I have warned you. For your advice. I thank you profoundly. And I wish you the utmost success in finding the Bigbee case."

His smile was open mockery; speech had given back to him his equilibrium of temper.

"You must not trouble yourself about that," said Creel. "The day after to-morrow before it is completely dark, I shall place the Bigbee case in responsible hands."

Ashe, who was turning to leave the room, halted an instant; but he shrugged his shoulders at once and walked away through the door.

CHAPTER IX

GARDEN TALK

THE MOST EXPERIENCED and courageous man of action might well have resigned himself to despair in the position of Andrew Creel, but the very fact that he had never before faced a crisis was now a help to him.

If it can be understood how nearly his former life had been an extended sleep, it can be taken for granted that on awakening he accepted the world as he found it. A place of peril, but for that very reason a place of infinite charm. It must not be imagined that he had found a scheme through which he could deliver himself from the power of Ashe and his companions, or that he forgot for one moment that the crisis awaited him at the little distance of two days.

But the two days themselves were as long as two eternities to the awakened senses of Creel. It seemed to him that he had never felt the warmth of sunshine before; every ticking second of the clock brought home a new delight to him; and in the place of certainty of escape he found consolation enough in an endless hope.

For that matter the criminal feels hope even while he sits in the electric chair awaiting the shock of the current. Oddly enough the greatest disturbing element for Creel was the expectation of the momentary arrival of the real Ormonde, the man who had awakened him, even if it were by chance, the man who had talked with him on the bow of the ship, the man who had raised his hand and made that odd, unconscious signal. For his coming would precipitate the final event which was now, by the decision of Ashe, postponed for two priceless days.

In the meantime he wished to be out under the keen, blue sky every waking moment, so on his first morning, after a breakfast which was served to him in his room, he sallied out into the little inner garden. For beside the broad sweeps of lawn and flowers and trees which ran over the rest of the peninsula, there was reserved a comparatively small walled place filled with shrubs and the choicest flowers. So far as he could tell, no one observed his movements and no effort was made to keep him within the house.

For a moment he stood with his head far back, fairly drinking the yellow sunlight which sent a warm tingling to the very tips of his fingers. Compared with all other air he had ever breathed, this was pure oxygen, pure stimulus. He drew down full breaths of it, like one who imbibes of the waters of eternal youth, as he sauntered down the first brick walk which presented itself. The garden was crisscrossed by these narrow little paths. They were very old walks, for almost everywhere the bricks were deeply hollowed by the tread of unnumbered feet, the edges were rounded, and through the cracks was a persistent growth of green things, grass or moss, which made an indescribably pleasant coloring with the red of the bricks. The garden wall, also, was of red bricks, though mostly completely covered by the growth of shrubs, but here and there charmingly revealed through the tangled lattice and lace work of a climbing vine. The corners of the garden were four bowers of greenery, which seemed hollow masses to the first glance of the eye. It was only by the merest accident that Creel discovered they might be anything else.

For as he walked along his foot struck on a pebble which scampered and bounced swiftly ahead of him and rolled on straight under the veil of one of these. Now the pebble was a rounded fragment of quartz, veined with bright colors, and as it had caught the eye of Creel he followed it idly, brushed aside the veil of leaves—and found within a perfect little arbor con-

taining a rustic seat, and in the seat was no less person than
Robert Lorrimer. He was engrossed in a large volume which
now lay upon both knees. The screen of leaves reduced the
sunlight to an ideal softness. He looked up with a start to the
face of Creel. The latter bowed and smiled, a rather grim, in-
scrutable smile.

He said: "In all my career, this is the most delicate compliment that has ever been paid me, but I don't know whether to
offer my thanks directly to you, sir, or to reserve them for Mr.
Ashe."

"Good morning," nodded Lorrimer. "But the compliment
of my presence—I suppose you refer to it—is due to the fine
morning, I'm afraid, and not to you."

"Tut, tut!" smiled Creel. "That is hardly worthy of you! But
I repeat that I'm deeply flattered. I knew, of course, that Ashe
intended to keep an eye upon me, but I never dreamed that the
formidable eye of Lorrimer himself would be reserved for that
purpose!"

At this a slight flush stained the cheek of Lorrimer, but it
disappeared at once, and settling back into his chair he smiled
kindly upon Creel. He said in that strange and husky voice:

"So you think I've been detailed to spy on you, Mr. Ormonde?
I'm sorry for that!"

"Not a bit; not a bit!" Creel assured him hastily. "There is
nothing for you to worry about, and I wish that you would
believe that your presence will not put me out in the least. I
should like to know, however, when the girl is expected to come
out into the garden."

"The girl?" repeated Lorrimer, frowning.

"Of course. Ashe knows I came here; he posted you in secret;
he will send out Anne Berwick; you will afterward report the
conversation which takes place between us."

"So you overheard us?" cried Lorrimer.

But Creel smiled benevolently down upon him and shook
his head.

"Bah!" growled Lorrimer. "It was merely a deduction, and I fell in with it like the veriest tyro. Well, well, we'll call the game off for this morning."

Here he made as if to rise, but Creel detained him with a gesture.

"Don't disturb yourself," he said. "There isn't the slightest reason for waiting until the stage should be set a second time, and as for audience, I could not ask for a better critic!"

And he pointed his little speech, with a profound bow.

Lorrimer chuckled softly. "Come," he said, "you're an amiable fellow, Ormonde, and I see you have the sense to hold no malice."

"Not the least particle," said Creel. "I am never angry with the Lord because he will not revise his creations, and you acted merely according to your nature. Also, I keep in mind a certain sense of policy which must have dictated to you the necessity of removing me from your midst. I formed the habit early of judging men for themselves and not for their relations with other men. I hope you appreciate the point."

"It is charmingly made," agreed Lorrimer, "and I hope it makes it possible for you to sit down and chat with me for a little time. To be frank, we did not expect you in the garden quite so early and it will probably be some little time before the girl appears. Gad, my dear fellow, it's a strange game you are playing. And will you actually make—er—advances to Anne under the very eye of Ashe?"

"It is he who is indiscreet," said Creel. "I warned him of the risk if he allowed me to see her. But, you see, there is a perverse element in the nature of Ashe. The height of the cliff tempts him to jump to destruction."

"You are very confident," murmured Lorrimer dryly.

"Thank you. The most valuable quality a man can have is a touch of that same confidence."

"But may I ask what on earth you expect to gain by making these almost—er—public advances to Anne? No, I won't ask you that. I'll only say, what is your guarantee that you will produce any impression on her in your decidedly—pardon me—limited time? But that's an awkward question. I've no wish to pry into the mysteries."

"My reason for hope," answered Creel, "is open to the eyes of any man. You see, Lorrimer, I trust in the strength of my love for her. That will work for me even through silence—even through stone walls."

Lorrimer regarded him with a caustic smile which gradually died away to an almost sad solemnity.

"My dear boy," he said, "my dear boy, I envy your optimism! Well, I honestly wish you happiness—and some success."

"Thank you."

"Yet I tremble for you when I think what courses Ashe might take if she were really moved by you. It would madden him, Ormonde. In fact, she is the one vulnerable spot in his nature. She is the heel of Achilles for him."

"At least," said Creel, "he must have forewarned her against me."

"You do him wrong," said Lorrimer with some warmth. "No, sir, that would violate Ashe's sense of honor."

"Really?"

"You are sarcastic, sir. But Ashe is a most remarkable fellow. He is fortified against you only by the shortness of the time in which you can operate. Pardon me again."

"Certainly. But tell me something more of the girl. Our acquaintanceship, you know, is—unusual, to say the least."

CHAPTER X

CREEL SOLVES A PROBLEM

"TO BE SURE," nodded Lorrimer, "and very romantic. As
I understand it, you never saw her in the flesh until yesterday.
You were fascinated by a photograph, learned her identity in a
most remarkable manner, discovered in an equally unusual way
how you might reach her, corresponded with her, and when you
learned of the impending death of her father, offered your aid.
Well, it sounds like the wildest romance."

"Doesn't it?" sighed Creel.

"Why, you say that as if I were telling you something new!"

"Everything we hear directly about ourselves seems new to
us," evaded Creel.

"That's true. And now about Anne? Dear girl! Well, it's odd
how she happens to be connected with us. The rest of us easily
slipped away from the notice of our relatives. Rincon and Kingston, of course, had none, and my own were easily satisfied that
I was out of the country. But Berwick found it difficult to
account for his frequent absences to his daughter. Finally she
traced him and reached him when he was in the midst of one
of our gatherings.

"You can imagine that it was most embarrassing. We were
bound to keep or destroy her. Yet, it was not easy to act against
a harmless girl. It was she who solved the difficulty. For after
she had learned something of our operations she was fascinated by the plans of the society. She has a brain like a man's
and the intuition of a woman added to it. She decided to join

53

her father in his rather unusual profession, and by Jove, she did! Not only joined us, but she has made a ripping success of it.

"It's true that she does not act very often, and that she will take no part in the deliberations of the council, but now and then when we have a peculiarly difficult bit of work ahead of us, we tell Anne about it, and nine times out of ten she goes out and wins. It was she who got the Bigbee case that her dog of a father afterward stole; but of course you know that."

Creel nodded, his eyes upon a misty distance.

"As a matter of fact," sighed Lorrimer, "there is only one case in which Anne has failed to solve the problem before us. It's a thing which has haunted us all for many months.

"At the very moment when you—ah—discovered me here, my friend, I was meditating the problem, but the solution is still before us."

He fixed a wistful eye upon Creel.

"If it were not for the—unfortunate—nature of our relations I would be tempted to lay our difficulty before you, Mr. Ormonde."

"Do so, by all means," said Creel, "for I must assure you, Mr. Lorrimer, that I rarely operate merely for personal gain. It is the problem for its own sake that fascinates me—the danger for its own sake— the chance attempted rather than the chance realized. So let me hear your difficulty."

Lorrimer stared for a moment, with uncertainty upon him. At last he said, with a sigh:

"I believe I could venture it. At least, there could be no resultant harm. I shall! This is the case. You will pardon me if I name no names."

"Certainly."

"A certain man of money owned largely—in several companies—great blocks of stock. At a time when he was well past sixty years old his first reverse struck him. Yes, after a life of singular good fortune, a period of misfortune began. It began with the death of his sister; then in turn his wife, his brother, his two nephews and his own single son died. Every one of his known relations was swept away by this holocaust within the space of two years.

"You already imagine what happened to the poor devil. He had been originally a man of keen affections. At first he was heartbroken by these losses. Finally he concentrated all his love on his money. It became not merely the power which it had been to him before—the means to varying ends—but a thing in itself delightful, soul-consuming.

"At about this time he suffered a slight reverse in the stock market. At once he became panic-stricken. He converted all his holdings, by degrees, into gold coin, and collected this treasure in his house, an old family heirloom. He became, in a word, a typical miser. It was very sad!"

Here Lorrimer paused to shake his head in commiseration.

"But no sooner did he have his money converted into gold than he was stricken with fear of every human being. He dismissed at a stroke all of his old servants; he hired new ones, and strove to keep them ignorant of his gold. He armed them against outside invasion.

"Now, it was about this time that we became aware of the true state of affairs in the house of the miser, and of course we immediately made an attempt. But why should I prolong the story through a long series of failures? It was I who directed the first attempt. It failed miserably. Then several others made plans. Ashe himself, whose genius in these affairs is unmistakable, failed completely.

"We turned the affair over to Anne, trusting in her womanly intuition to find a means, and she also was at a loss. The brain of the old miser is sharpened past belief by the love for his gold. He surrounds it with a thousand guards; it seems impregnable.

"Now he is passing rapidly into a decline; his death approaches; his gold will be turned over to the State, owing to the lack of heirs, and the priceless opportunity—for I assure

you that the sum involved is astonishingly large—is snatched
forever from our hands."

He had grown increasingly emphatic toward the close of his
narrative, and in the end was trembling and flushed with excitement. Now he leaned back and laughed hoarsely.

"You see," he said, "the effect that the mere telling of the tale
has upon me. Ormonde, there are times when I'm half mad
over the problem. But there is no solution. We've already made
so many attempts that the man actually knows some of our
faces, and probably has more information about our society
than any other living human being. Not only that, but his information has enabled him to put the police twice upon our
trail, and both times they ran dangerously close to the mark.

"In fact, both times they succeeded in seizing upon a member—a lesser member of the organization, to be sure. Both were
guilty of capital offenses; both chose death rather than a be-
trayal of the society. But think of the danger that threatens us
so long as this infernal old skinflint clings to his life—and his
gold. Well, Ormonde, have you anything to suggest?"

"Certainly," replied Creel instantly; and it seemed to him
that the words were placed upon his tongue by an exterior
influence, for the instant before his brain had been a blank.
"There is this to be borne in mind, Mr. Lorrimer. Everything
has two viewpoints. One from the inside, and one from the
outside."

He leaned back. The power had him in its grip; he was talking
like a medium, hardly conscious of the words he uttered. It was
as if some one sat at his side and repeated the phrases for him
to imitate. He went on:

"You have been looking at this case from the outside; seeing
merely your desire to get the gold; seeing the danger of losing
it which will come to you when the old man dies. Now I want
you to look at this case from the inside, something which is
often of the greatest value to me. Consider the old man. He is
haunted day and night by fear. Each time he repulses one of

your attempts he feels no joy. He is stabbed to the heart by terror; he feels that his yellow gold, his horde, his beautiful river of money, has almost been snatched from him, as so many other things have been snatched in the past. The worry has stretched him on his deathbed, and that death will rob him both of the money and you of all hope of it. And now what do you do? You go to him and say:

"You know me. You know my face; you know that I am one of a powerful organization which is concentrating on an attempt to tear your gold away from you. We have hitherto failed, but can you be sure that we will not succeed one of these days? You cannot. And you are stretched on your bed with terror.

" 'Now, hear the bargain we will make with you. We will guarantee that not one of our order will touch a cent of your money while you are alive. We will further furnish you with men who are familiar with the men and the ways of the criminal world, and they will guarantee your safety from the attempts of other thieves. As long as you live you will have your gold to delight you. You can bathe in it if you wish. You can carry it up from your dark places and let the sun strike upon it. And in return you merely make out your will in favor of me. As long as you live the gold is yours. When you die, when it is no more to you than so much lead, it shall come into our possession. You shall live and die in peace, and we shall be rich hereafter. Both parties gain by the contract.'

"Mr. Lorrimer, make that proposition!"

"By God," cried Lorrimer, starting to his feet, "I believe he would do it. But, no—he is dying now. He knows that he must die. He will laugh at me."

"I am forced to smile," said Creel dryly. "Of course the man is dying, but he still has hope. Revive that hope, and he will *think* that he is reviving. You have only to make sure that he has made out the will in the correct terms—and be sure that you divide the money equally among your companions."

"And you—" began Lorrimer, casting out his arms in a

gesture of sudden gratitude. Then he checked himself, flushing and biting his lips.

"As for me," smiled Creel, "you may see that flowers are always kept fresh upon my grave. Or am I to be favored with a grave?"

"However that may be," said Lorrimer, "and unfortunately it lies in the hands of Ashe to decide, and not in mine, I assure you, sir, that I shall use the utmost of my efforts to save you. Will you believe me?"

"From the bottom of my heart, and thank you," said Creel carelessly.

"In the name of God," cried Lorrimer, "do you really think that you are in no actual danger?"

"To tell you the truth," said Creel, "I see the danger, but I do not feel it."

Lorrimer remained standing, staring incredulously.

"Sir," he said at length, "what you are I cannot say, but at least you are like no other man on God's green earth. Mr. Ormonde, I take off my hat to a great genius!"

And suiting his action to his word, he removed his wide-brimmed hat and bowed almost to the ground.

"You are very kind," said Creel, "but now I must leave you, for there, if I mistake not, comes the lady I must meet."

CHAPTER XI

ANNE BERWICK

"IN THAT CASE," said Lorrimer, "I assure you that I shall see no more than I have to in order to report to Ashe. And I wish you luck."

"For that," replied Creel, "I thank you indeed."

And he stepped out from the screen of shrubbery, and went down the walk toward the house.

She wore a dress of filmy blue, of a material which he did not recognize, and now she leaned above a little border of pinks and picked them. One hand was held out behind her as if to balance her in the posture, and the fingers of the other hand seemed almost transparent in the sunshine. The brightness which she had carried into the dim room the day before was doubly apparent here, for the sun lay in her hair like fire, and the wind ruffled at her dress as if it had blown her that moment into the garden and might in an instant pick her up again and hurry her far away.

Straightening, she regarded the little bunch of pinks with a faint smile of satisfaction, and then walked on slowly. She was humming a tune so lightly that the beat and rhythm of it rather than the actual music came to Creel. And he followed her pace for pace, soft-footed as a shadow. All at once she came to an abrupt halt and then whirled and faced him, keen-eyed, alert, as if she expected and was ready to repel a swift attack from behind.

At sight of Creel she started again, and cried out with a note of happiness that went thrilling through him:

"They have set you free again? Is it all well again?"

And she went to him—yes, though he could hardly believe it—she almost ran to him and caught both his hands. Perhaps it was the light wind blowing her dress, but as she stood with her eyes shining into his, she seemed to lean a little toward him. Creel was very pale, and he stood very stiff and straight. He had been educated in a military school, and that old habit of standing at attention came back to him always when he was deeply moved.

She was speaking, but he was drowned in the sight of her, in the very sound of the voice, fascinated by the catch and hurry of her breathing. She poured like wine upon him from a magic and exhaust-less flask. The words themselves were dim and colorless things. They had no value, save that she had spoken them. He knew in that moment what he had known the day before, but had not allowed to come into his sentient brain: he had seen that face before and loved it.

It was no new love: it was old; it was like an instinct inherited from a former life. He had stepped in a second through the dusky flight of centuries and stood there with her in a new-old age.

But this was what she said:

"When I saw you yesterday I didn't dare smile on you; hardly dared look at you. Ashe is a devil in jealousy; I was afraid. Afterward I sat in my room, thinking it all over and gradually realizing or trying to realize the horrible truth—that you were sentenced to death in two days. And then—I couldn't stand it. I went down to Ashe and begged him—on my knees. He—he wouldn't answer me—and then he turned and walked out of the room without saying a word, and I thought—"

But here the flood of words was stopped by a little, sharp, almost discordant cry of happiness.

"No matter what I thought! Here you are—free—in the sunshine—with me!"

His voice trembled like his body. He said huskily:

"Let's sit here—this bench. I just want to look—and look—and see you!"

And there they were sitting; and she still held both his hands. And she said—he heard the words now like the most marvelous music:

"Did you think that last letter of mine a shameless thing? I couldn't help it! I sat down before the paper with your letter beside me, and the words simply came all by themselves."

"They were beautiful words," he said in hardly more than a whisper.

"And only five of them! But you knew that it was more than mere gratitude for saving my father that made me write them?"

"I prayed that it might be so," he murmured, eyes kindling.

She said in that indescribable low voice which took hold on him like a hand which was like an electric touch, like a flash in utter darkness:

"Edward Ormonde! Turn your head so that I can see you, Edward Ormonde!"

Oh, the bitterness of it! To receive such love, to feel it as strongly as a physical force, to be carried along on the flood of it like straw on a mighty river, and to know that it was meant for another man—for Edward Ormonde!

He recalled the picture of Ormonde—the alert eyes, the slightly compressed, nervous mouth. Yes, there was a man who could write poetry, whose passion even in his letters could have kindled such an answering fire as this which sat beside him, burned him, illumined him.

He said: "To-day let the fire burn; to-morrow I shan't regret the ashes."

"What do you mean?" she asked.

"Nothing! Nothing! Anne, Anne, talk to me!"

"What shall I say?"

"Anything—everything! Talk to me! Tell me you love me; just talk, and shut out the rest of the world with your words. Anne, for the first time I am living—all of me! Tell me—yes, tell me what it was made you first dream you could love me?"

"I can tell you the very words. They're graven in me. It was a sentence in one of your first letters. Do you remember how I wrote, asking you why you didn't give up your life? Why you didn't turn all your power into some legitimate course? And you answered a thing that lighted up your whole character for me. I saw you before simply as other men I knew—men who destroyed for the love of destroying and for personal gain. You answered what I had felt myself. These are the words: 'It is the problem for its own sake that fascinates me—the danger for its own sake—the chance attempted rather than the chance realized.'"

"Did I say that?" asked Creel, stunned. For he remembered what he had said only a few moments ago to Lorrimer. "Dear Heaven, did I say that?"

"What is wrong?"

"Nothing, Anne! Good Heaven! What has happened? What *is* happening? Look at me! Tell me my name!"

"Edward Ormonde! What is it? I'm afraid—almost as if—as if you were a stranger!"

"Edward Ormonde," he repeated, and then fiercely: "Edward Ormonde. Tell me—didn't you almost recognize me the moment you set eyes on me?"

"I did."

"And it was like a power set on you—a hand reaching out to you?"

"Yes, yes! Was it that way with you?"

"That way with me also. I don't understand—nothing except that we belong to each other—all of us!"

And she murmured: "Oh, my dear!"

She was leaning to him, swaying, and then she was in his

arms, but the touch startled him back to cold reality. He disengaged himself; he stood before her in the path. And she looked up at him, wide-eyed, dazed.

He said: "I was mad to do that—to touch you. Anne, we are watched by one of Ashe's men!"

That brought her to her feet beside him. She swept the garden with a terrified glance.

"I knew that he would never let us be alone together," he went on. "And I feared that he might never even let you see me a second time. So I taunted him. I dared him, in a way, to let me meet you only once, and swore that I would destroy all his influence over you. And he accepted the chance; he allowed me to come here—arranged it so that you would come—and planted a man to overlook us. And now—"

She reached out to him, but he caught her hands and drew them down.

"Don't touch me, Anne. I'm lost already, and only a little more and your father will be lost also. Don't you see? Ashe hasn't relented. The sentence still hangs over me."

"It can't!" she cried. "I'll go to him; I'll beg again; I'll promise him—"

"Nothing!" ordered Creel sternly. "Do you hear me? You'll promise nothing! Anne, it couldn't save me, and I'd rise from my grave to haunt you. But you can save your father if you follow the right course. It all depends. Let Ashe think for an instant that you are truly in love with me, and your father dies to-morrow. Let him think that he has the ghost of a hope, and your father will live. Do you follow me?"

"I do—I try to follow you."

"Then play your cards for your father."

"But you, Edward—oh God—you and I?" she sobbed.

"I only know one thing," he answered. "Something stronger than human has taken us in hand. And I trust to it."

CHAPTER XII

THE STRENGTH OF THE WEAK

THAT BELIEF HAD grown up in him swiftly in the last few minutes. It was now a strong consciousness. That he should have solved the problem of Lorrimer so easily was in itself strange; that he should have spoken in the identical words of Edward Ormonde was more than strange. It passed at a step beyond the common.

One instance was enough for wonder; two such instances carried him at once into the region of the supernatural. And not these two concrete instances alone—there was also that inexplicable change, that awakening since his first meeting with Ormonde—since his very first sight of him—and above all was the singular impression of familiarity which Anne made upon him. All these things, tumbling about confusedly in his brain, made him almost happy when Anne left him. He went at once to his room and sat down to bring the confusion to order.

What came from it in the end was not, oddly enough, fear for himself, but fear for Anne. But when he opened the door into the hall a fellow with a skin of Egyptian darkness sauntered up to him and shook his head.

"So this is their decision?" asked Creel.

In place of answering, his guard dropped a hand to a hip pocket and stood in watchful silence, like one prepared to resist any sudden and desperate effort.

"And silent, too?" queried Creel. "Well, I wish you a pleasant day, my friend."

"Listen to me, bo," said the other, speaking rapidly and from the corner of his mouth. "Don't make no funny play. I know you're a bad 'un, but it ain't no coin in your pocket even if you get past me. There's others watchin' you." He stepped closer, and his voice became a hissing whisper. "It's the big guy himself that is knifing you."

"Thank you," answered Creel; "but I could have guessed that before."

And when he had closed his door he crossed the room and looked down from the window on the opposite side. The sweep of lawn beneath was paced by no guardian, but after a moment of inspection he made out the form of a man pacing unostentatiously to and fro among the trunks of a little grove of pine trees.

After that he sat down and remained perfectly quiet during almost the entire remainder of the day. His mind was the more active for the passivity of his body, for he was concentrating steadily on a problem of linking Edward Ormonde and himself and James Ashe together. It had come to him out of thin air that in that combination lay in some mysterious manner the knowledge which would enable him to extricate both himself and Anne. At this puzzle he worked. This was the thin plate of steel which held him back from all the treasure of life itself and of Anne. His fingers were on the combination which would open the door, but he had lost the numbers.

Lunch and dinner were in turn served to him in the silence of his room, and still he concentrated on the puzzle. No wonder, then, that he suddenly started up when there was a faint click from the door to his room. It opened, and James Ashe himself entered. There was no greeting. There was no delay; he went directly to the point.

"Mr. Creel," he said, "I have decided that it is better for my interests that you be given your liberty. I am about to set you free. The only thing I ask in return is a guarantee that you will keep silence concerning the society. Your mere promise will do;

and what you know of the power of the society, I am sure, will keep you from chattering."

"Ah," answered Creel, "you've been through my effects. And you're quite confident that my name is Creel?"

"Perfectly confident. Creel or not, the important thing is that you are not Ormonde. Even if you were Ormonde, it would not help you. The members agree with me that your coming here without the Bigbee case"—here his shadow of a smile returned—"is too mysterious. They fear that you have a double purpose, and agree that there is danger. They propose to meet that danger by putting an immediate end to it. Is it plain?"

"Quite plain, thank you."

"But for my own personal ends your death would be an inconvenience, for reasons into which I do not care to enter. Give me your promise to be discreet after you leave the place, and I shall provide you with means of exit. A key and a password are all that you need. I have them both here for you. Quick, Creel! I am expected below."

But Creel observed him with a gradually growing smile. It seemed to madden Ashe, but he restrained himself with an effort that left him pale.

"You must know that it's perfectly impossible for me to leave in this summary manner. There is a person here who might—"

"I have provided for that," answered Ashe. "Here is a note for you."

Creel took it and read:

> It is all too impossible. It began in nothing; it should end in nothing. There is no other way. For my sake, accept the offer of Mr. Ashe, and go.
>
> ANNE.

This he tore with care into tiny portions, and then tossed the bits into a little fireplace at the side of the room.

"Now, isn't it strange," he said at length to Ashe, "that a woman can transform a man? You, Ashe, are normally brave, and normally—according to your standards—decent. But the girl has changed you to a coward and a cur."

The desire for murder was in the eye of Ashe, but the only physical action which replied to the taunt was a spasmodic contraction of his right hand.

"So you went to her and tried to buy her at the price of my safety? Ashe, that is low—very low indeed."

"It is her proposition from beginning to end," replied Ashe. "Take it or leave it. For my part, I already begin to regret that I have made it to you."

"I shall not take it," said Creel.

Ashe started again.

"Are you quite mad?" he asked. "I tell you, the only thing which can buy your freedom is the Bigbee case. Every member is agreed with that proposition."

"Then probably I shall have the case in time."

"On that question you seem absolutely mad. I assure you—" He broke off and added, rather hastily: "Then I have to leave you to another twenty-four hours of hell waiting for your end?"

"Twenty-four hours of hell? No, twenty-four hours of study. I am working on a very interesting case. Another thing, Ashe. It is absolutely impossible for me to fear you, whereas it is absolutely impossible for you not to fear me."

"I?" cried Ashe. "I fear you?"

"Yes; the twenty-four hours of hell belong to you. For every minute of that time you will be pondering on what effect my death will have on Anne. By the Lord, Ashe, I almost pity you. I am the barrier between you and her, and yet by removing me you erect a still greater barrier."

"Time," muttered Ashe, his forehead gleaming with perspiration, "will remove any barrier."

"Do you think so?" replied Creel quietly. "Do you honestly think so, Ashe?"

"Damn you!" answered Ashe. "And damn the hour that brought you here!"

"And yet," went on Creel, "you have now gone too far to draw back. Already your shielding of Berwick for the sake of the girl has shaken your hold over the society, and if you venture to protect me also your fall will be close at hand. You know it, and greatly as you value the girl, you value your power still more. It is hard, Ashe. By my soul, I almost pity you in fact!"

"If this is all you can answer," said Ashe, still deadly white, "I will leave you, Mr. Creel."

"And think," continued Creel, "how you have even fought to prove to Anne that I am not Ormonde. You are confident of the fact. You have placed in her hands all the documents of proof which you gleaned from my effects, and yet she only laughed at you; at every pause in your proof that I am Creel and not Ormonde she begged you once more to assure my safety. In the end she promised everything as the price of my security."

"So you've seen her since I left her?" said Ashe, his face contorting with malevolence. "Some one shall pay richly for this!"

"You are wrong again," answered Creel. "I read it all in your baffled face, Ashe. I read it in the lines about your mouth, in the shadows beneath your eyes which prove that you did not sleep last night and that you will not sleep to-night. I read it all, and, as I said before, I almost pity you, Ashe."

"I want none of it. For the last time, Creel: will you accept safety and freedom, or will you die miserably at dark to-morrow?"

"And she is a great deal to lose," went on Creel. "There is not her like. Isn't she like sunshine and a fresh wind, Ashe? Aye, the thought of losing her would put shadows under my eyes also!"

But Ashe turned on his heel and fairly fled from the room.

CHAPTER XIII

THE COMING OF THE DARK

AFTER ASHE LEFT him it became impossible for Creel to worry. The problem of the three names was still before him, but now he could not fight with it. The weight of it was lifted from him by invisible hands, and he was filled with an almost religious trust that in the crisis the solution would be put in his mind. The same calm certainty allowed him to sleep like a child that night and it stayed with him the next day.

Only when the sun passed the zenith and the shadows fell more and more slanting from the trees and across the bright green of the lawn, a doubt rose and grew stronger with the passing of each moment; for when the darkness came on Windon Manor he was to die.

And how could even some impalpable connection between himself, Ormonde, and Ashe save him? To be sure, it was only when he tried to reason it out that he became depressed. If he allowed his mind to remain careless, all trouble fled from him. And now the sunset came and over Windon Manor fell a deepening shadow.

A knock came at his door, and he opened it to Lorrimer. His manner was never more gracious.

"I have come like the raven with ill tidings," he said, after he had greeted Creel. "Mr. Ashe is waiting for you in the garden."

"Very good," nodded Creel, and stepped obediently into the hall.

"And I must ask you, Mr. Ormonde," said Lorrimer, following, "to walk before me—and slowly. It is unnecessary for me to warn you that I am armed. I'm sorry to begin with all these precautionary statements."

"Don't trouble about that," said Creel cheerfully.

"To say that we all regret the necessity of this step," went on the smooth, low voice of Lorrimer, "would be to understate the truth. And we still have a hope that at the last moment it will turn out that you have been simply testing our firmness, and will produce the Bigbee case. For we have certain information, Mr. Ormonde, that it was in your hands when you left England.

"In the meantime, I know you will be delighted to learn that your little stratagem has succeeded perfectly with the old fellow about whom I talked with you yesterday morning. Yes, I myself went to him, and before last night the will was made out in satisfactory terms—highly satisfactory. Thinking of this, Mr. Ormonde, I know that if the worst comes to the worst you will fall like Samson in the midst of a great deed."

"You are kind," muttered Creel.

"The very simplicity of your plan," continued Lorrimer, "has made some of our associates undervalue it, but I have convinced them that all worthwhile things are essentially simple. And here we are at the garden, Mr. Ormonde."

He held the door open, adding as Creel passed out: "And if things turn out for the best, Mr. Ormonde, I want you to know that I held you to the last in the highest esteem and respect—the very highest, sir."

And Creel's last sight was of him standing in the open door, rubbing his long, pale hands together. He went down the steps and straight up one of the narrow brick paths, for at the farther end of the garden he saw Ashe. The big man was pacing up and down in violent agitation. At sight of Creel he stopped short and faced him, and Creel saw what a havoc the last day had worked on the face of the man.

He said: "Creel, the sun is down, but there are still a few minutes before the darkness comes. When it is so dark that I cannot make out the color of the flowers in the garden, you die. But there is still a moment left in which you can change your mind. And listen! If you decide at once I think that I can still save you. Flee, Creel, and—who knows?—you may find some means of reaching Anne afterward. But if you wait for half an hour you die miserably. Creel, that is as fixed as the stars in heaven!"

It would be hard to tell how Creel might have answered that proposal, for with the coming of the dark at Windon Manor life grew inexpressibly sweet to him; simply to live one more day and feel once more the sunshine was in itself a great end for which a thousand lesser things might have been sacrificed. But it happened that in glancing up, hesitant, his eyes struck on a window of the manor, and beyond the pane was a glimmer of white which he knew to be the watching face of Anne Berwick. How she had managed to come there he could not guess. And perhaps she dared not give any open sign of her presence, for fear Ashe would have her taken away again. But she was there. He could not distinguish a single feature, but he knew perfectly that it was she.

"I will wait for the darkness," Ashe said, "at the farther end of the garden, Ormonde."

And with that he turned and walked slowly back.

Creel sat down on a bench under the black shadow of the house, and looking out from this deep night the evening over the garden still seemed as bright as midday, almost. But it changed and faded swiftly; the bright roses on the climbing vine along the wall were blurred with trailing, deepening shades; and the breath of the flowers held a funereal sweetness for Creel.

That dimness of the flowers recalled him suddenly to Ashe, and when his eyes fell upon the man he started up with a slight cry. For Ashe, continuing his restless pacing up and down the paths, was now walking away from Creel, and seemed about to disappear into the gloom of the late twilight.

Seen in this manner, his shoulders were singularly broad and

massive, and he carried his head far to one side, a thoughtful
cant. And then the whole solution of the riddle came home to
Creel. He saw it all in a flash, and with the joy that went flood-
ing through heart and brain he wanted to shout aloud.

Instead he walked swiftly up to Ashe and touched his shoulder. The man turned without a word, and even through that
dim light Creel made out the ghastly hollows of the other's
eyes.

"Mr. Ashe," he said, "there are still a few moments left to
me, for see, we can make out that lily quite clearly, and I am to
live until the darkness is complete over Windon Manor. So let's
pass the last moments in some friendly talk. The silence weighs
upon me."

"Talk, for God's sake!" muttered Ashe, "It weighs upon me
also."

"I wonder," answered Creel, "if you have ever paid much
attention to theories of reincarnation?"

"Such nonsense as that," said Ashe, "has never occupied me
for a moment."

"And yet," said Creel, "there is something fascinating about
it. The point on which I have always stuck, however, is that the
soul of a man should remain bodiless for an indefinite period
and then enter in with the formation of a new body. Now it
seems much more, feasible, for instance, that the soul of a man,
upon death, should actually dispossess the soul of another man
who is still living."

"I don't understand you."

"No; it seems too unearthly. But suppose a man whose mind
and will and purposes have never been developed. Suppose a
man whose life presents a blank slate. Now consider another
man's instinct with strength and energy. Suppose a man so vital
that his very nearness to this first formless mind would thrill
it with an instinct of life, awaken it as another man might be
awakened from sleep by a calling voice. Now, then, is it conceivable that if the strong man should die those unfulfilled pur-

poses of his would crave action, and his soul would literally take possession of the weaker man? Would it not be conceivable that the soul of the dead man might literally usurp the body of the living man and go on living in that new shell?"

"Conceivable," I suppose," said Ashe, "but damned foolish."

"Perhaps. Nevertheless, it is my firm conviction, Mr. Ashe, that the soul of dead Edward Ormonde is now living again in me!"

For an instant Ashe was silent, and then he broke into soft laughter.

"You admit openly, then, that you are not Ormonde?"

"Certainly—to you."

"And you think that Ormonde himself is dead?"

"Listen," said Creel, "and I will tell you a little story. It concerns yourself. When you received word that Edward Ormonde was about to attempt to regain possession of the Bigbee case which Berwick had lost and thereby forfeited his life to your society—when you knew, I say, that Edward Ormonde himself was going to attempt to regain that case, and as a reward for his services obtain the freedom of Berwick and perhaps get Anne as his reward, you went mad with jealousy, eh?"

"Go on with your story," said Ashe coldly. "And be quick. I can still see the lily, but it is as faint as a ghost."

"To be sure! Well, then, I say you were mad with jealousy, and you decided that you must get to England and prevent Edward Ormonde from returning with the Bigbee case. You sailed at once without informing the society, of course, of your destination. Your search in England was in vain, till at the last moment you got on the right trail and followed Ormonde onto the ship in which he was starting for America with the case. On the ship you waited for your opportunity, and it came the night before the ship entered New York Harbor. It was the dim time of the evening—"

"Damn you!" whispered Ashe fervently, and made a step forward.

Creel thrust his hand into an inner coat and knotted it into a fist, so that it might appear he grasped something.

"Stand your ground and keep your distance, Ashe," he warned, "or I'll send you to hell a little before your time. I'm armed!"

"Who gave you a gun?" snarled Ashe. "Ah, there's the hand of Anne in this!"

"You are wrong again. Ashe, you are weak in quarters which you never suspect. But to continue. You stole out on the bow of the ship, but for a time you were prevented from approaching Ormonde, who stood talking with a man whose face you could not see in the darkness. At length he went away, and then you went straight to Ormonde, came upon him from behind—"

"You lie like a dog! I met him face to face—"

"Good! In one detail I accept correction. You throttled his outcry; one grip of your hands was enough; then you dropped the body overboard. Afterward you went to his cabin—"

"Creel!" cried Ashe in a voice altered past recognition. "In the name of God—"

"And now," broke in Creel, "do you believe? Am I Edward Ormonde?"

"No. Thank God, he is dead. Do you hear? Dead, dead, dead!"

"You fool! Listen to me! Don't you hear his voice in me? Can't you feel the working of his mind? Could this mind of Andrew Creel have solved the problem for Lorrimer? No, it is Edward Ormonde. But you know it! In spite of the dimness I see your color fade. Ashe, you're afraid. But you're not facing a ghost. At least, it's a ghost in the form of a man. And as a man I demand the thing that you have about you—the Bigbee case, Ashe! Hand it over!"

There was such a moment of pause as comes when two bodies are rushing together—the moment of waiting for the crash; and then Creel knew that Ashe would not fight.

He said rapidly:

"Quick! For if I should call—if I should demand that you

be examined—if they should find the case upon you, what would become of you? If they should learn that you are betraying them, trying like Berwick to cheat them of their share of the spoils—"

"Creel, if I had taken the case from Ormonde, do you dream I would carry it about with me?"

"What could be a better place? A thing of that value you would not dare to trust even in a steel safe. Ashe, hand me the case intact, or I swear I shall call your own men out to search you. Do you hear? I tell you, I *know* that you have it!"

And Ashe, staring like one under hypnotic influence, slowly thrust his hand into a breast pocket and placed in the extended fingers of Creel a gun-metal case. It was like a cigarette case in size, and like a cigarette case it opened by the pressure on a snap. From within, bedded in velvet, a dim glow of light, like the glitter of many eyes, came out to Creel. He closed the case again with a click.

"And now," he said, "it only remains that we go in together, side by side, to face your comrades. The tragedy is ended—at least for me. We appear before them and tell them that I have had the case concealed about my person all this time, and that I have simply been testing the strength of will of the society. And then—"

"Aye, and one thing more—and if you were Ormonde himself you would shrink from doing that. It is an oath of membership in the society, an oath which makes you one of us, sworn by everything man holds sacred to aid us when you are called upon—to join us when you are summoned—to value us more than child or family. Have you thought of that, my friend Creel?"

Once more Creel paused, and once more, looking up to the window in his distress, he saw the face of Anne Berwick, a mere touch of white beyond the pane. He would be free to take her now. But how? He must take her as Ormonde—a king of thieves, but nevertheless a thief. He must bind himself as a member of the criminal world. He must condemn himself to a perpetual servitude in crime. But she was the reward which the oath would bring him. His mind was made up.

"That," he said to Ashe, "is a simple thing. Look up, Ashe. She is standing behind that window, and she is waiting for me already."

"Damn you again," said Ashe in a broken voice of hate and pain. "But in the end you will have to reckon with me still, Ormonde. Yes, and in the end I'll have my hands at your throat a second time, and that will finish you. Now I'm beaten; but it's only for the moment. To-day is yours; to-morrow is mine. Remember that. The cup of wine is in your hand. The thought of me shall be the poison in it!"

"Spoken man to man," said Creel, "and in the end I know we shall meet again. Then God have mercy upon one of us! But now, Mr. Ashe, it is very dark. I cannot see the color of the flowers."

It was not a full ten minutes later that the society heard, and saw, and believed. For indeed the jewels of the Bigbee case were eloquent. And it was not quite ten minutes later still that Creel stood with his hand upon an open book with the echo of his own late spoken words ringing through his mind. And when he looked up it was only to meet the smiling malice of Robert Lorrimer and the cold eye of Matthew Kingston—an oddly hungry eye. But he shrugged his shoulders, and the thought of the future fell away from him. Who will think of the storm that rages about him when the glow of an open and hospitable door is directly before him?

"And now," he said, "I am free?"

"Free as the wind," answered Ashe, "until you are needed."

"Then," said Creel, "I bid you a very good night."

And as he made for the door he felt the eye of Ashe following him.

Word had already been carried to her. Perhaps a servant had brought it. For as he ran up the stairs toward that room whose windows overlooked the garden he heard a little, sharp, almost discordant cry above him, and, looking up, he saw her hurrying down to him. The glow from the hall light was full upon her face. But even in the joy of that meeting Creel felt, somehow, the cold eye of Ashe upon him.

CHAPTER XIV

DOUBT

A ROADSTER STOOD at the door of Windon Manor, a heavy car and low hung. Its excessive length made it graceful in spite of its bulk; even as it stood still it suggested breathless speed, and the big gasoline tank behind added a connotation of distance.

Even to the novice's eye of Creel it was a fine machine, and he walked about it slowly, much as a gambler views the thoroughbred in the paddock before the race. He and Anne Berwick wore going to New York in that car. Creel glanced up along the road and then shrugged the overcoat closer about his shoulders.

It was still the chill of the morning; the new-risen sun lay behind thick drifts of mist; his light flooded the zenith, but all the earth was dim. Under the tall trees of Windon Manor lingered the night; a heavy dew glittered on the lawn; the gravel of the driveway was dark with moisture. Beyond the hills faint columns of smoke rose straight up in the stirless air. The hush of dark held over into the morning, and the few signs of life merely served to exaggerate the quiet.

Only the birds were fully awake, and their singing dropped in far, sweet choruses from the light of the upper air. While Creel stood with his head back to listen he heard a footfall crunching the gravel and turned to find Robert Lorrimer.

He was returning from a before-breakfast stroll. He wore knickerbockers, a short, plaid jacket of some heavy woolen stuff, brightly colored; thick stockings, and low shoes. The long visor of his cap exaggerated the sharpness of his features, and the red of his jacket matched the flush of his cheeks. He looked like a compromise between youth and age.

Creel studied his approach with quiet amusement, for through Lorrimer he would learn what attitude the men of Windon Manor were about to assume toward him. The day before they had been keenly bent on his destruction. Through a miracle, or a near miracle, he had been saved, and was now admitted to the inner heart of the society and bound to it with terrific oaths. He could not help wondering how they would reconcile their former attitude with his present position.

Robert Lorrimer waved his hand and hallooed from the distance. He came to a halt before Creel, breathing hard. He held his watch in his hand.

"A three-mile turn in thirty-two minutes!" he explained exultantly, and held out his watch as though it could verify his statement. "How is that for an old fellow?" And he removed his cap and passed his fingers through the silver mist of hair.

"Better time than I could make," nodded Creel.

The tall man slapped him merrily on the shoulder.

"Ormonde, you sly dog," he grinned, "we know you better than you think. You'd have me making a match with you, but I tell you I've heard the strength of those meager limbs of yours. Fifteen years ago I wouldn't have dodged you, but today—"

He paused and sighed deeply. "However," he went on more gayly, "I may be an old man at high noon, but I'll still be young till the prime of the day. It's the heart that counts, Ormonde, and my heart is as young as two-and-twenty, upon my word. There's a great deal of the child in me, my lad, you'd never guess how much! Why, this very morning, over the crest of that hill there, I stopped for a good ten minutes and watched a gopher at work—a busy little devil—and I paused for another five minutes and watched a crow tilting on the top of a bush as solemn as you please—"

"And yet," broke in Creel, "with fifteen minutes of rest you managed the three miles in thirty-two minutes? Gad, Lorrimer, you're a champion!"

"I took the time out," replied Lorrimer instantly. "I took the time out most carefully, but by the Lord, sir, with your eye for accuracy you miss the chief joy of your young days. Open your heart, Ormonde! More abandon! You remember far too exactly."

"However," smiled Creel, "I have my memory under control and can forget when I wish."

Lorrimer regarded him soberly for an instant.

"I think I follow your meaning," he said, and his sharp scrutiny went deeply into the eyes of Creel. "The dead may bury their dead, eh—and bygones may be bygones? Will you give me your hand on that, Ormonde?"

A strong revulsion in the face of this profound hypocrite made Creel set his teeth; he controlled himself with an effort.

"A handshake," he said, "is a pledge, and I dodge pledges. However, a very good morning to you, Lorrimer." And he shook hands with a firm grip.

"You're a subtle fellow," remarked Lorrimer with a rather wan smile. "For my part, I'm blunt and open. A child may read me like a book. Well, I pay the penalty for too much frankness, so let it go at that."

But Creel broke into laughter, hearty, uncontrolled. Lorrimer observed him with a growing gleam of understanding.

"No more of this," he said quietly at length, "but don't judge me too harshly, Ormonde."

"I assure you," answered Creel, "that this is another day of school, and I've quite rubbed out the old lesson. Have you noticed how the trees keep the night over Windon Manor? Everywhere else it is morning light—look at that hill!—but here we're under a shadow, eh?"

"There may be a double meaning in that," said Lorrimer thoughtfully; and then he picked up the new clew gladly enough and went on: "But you have your particular sunshine coming down to you, Ormonde. Anne is taking you out for a spin?"

"We're running over to New York."

"She drives like the wind—a veritable storm wind, at that. But I forget that you're one of these speed lovers yourself. I know about your drive from Glasgow to Woolwich, and I suppose you'll find even Anne slow. Well, joy be with you. For my part, I'd rather travel in a catboat through a simoon than ride a mile beside Anne Berwick's wheel."

"H-m!" murmured Creel with a singular lack of enthusiasm.

"Her last car," reflected Lorrimer, "she liked better than this; but it was an English make, and she couldn't duplicate it."

"She wore it out?" asked Creel a trifle anxiously.

"It skidded on a turn," answered the other, "and smashed into another car. She was doing fifty miles, and the street was wet, you see."

"Good God!" burst out Creel.

"Nobody killed," said Lorrimer. "One broken collar bone and a dislocated hip. Anne was thrown through the windshield and landed on the pavement, but she came out with only a few bruises. She couldn't get a car like the one that was wrecked, and—"

"But fifty miles—how—" stammered Creel.

"How did she escape with her neck? It was a rear collision. The other car was going the same way she was traveling. Also, she probably had only two wheels on the ground when she struck."

Creel loosened his collar.

"Of course," he suggested, "that accident slowed up Anne's driving a bit?"

"Not at all," said Lorrimer, shaking his head with decision. "She attributed the skidding to the fact that the treads were pretty well worn down on her rear tires. Always has a reason for everything that happens, you know. When she smashed that other racer through the fence—"

"What?" gasped Creel.

"I thought you might have heard of that. Ancient history. She was doing about sixty on a straight road and took both hands off the wheel to adjust her hat. The car swerved to one side, jumped a ditch, clipped off a fence post, and lodged in some plowed ground on the other side. Also, it was the softness of the plowed ground that broke the force of Anne's fall."

"And what," queried Creel faintly, "was the reason she gave for that?"

"We all wondered what she would have to say. She told us that any automobile that's worthy of the name should run straight on a smooth road without much working of the wheel."

"But why," cried Creel in indignation, "doesn't some one control her?"

Lorrimer turned full upon him and regarded him in wide-eyed amazement.

"Control?" he asked. "Control Anne?" He added dryly: "If you are going to do that, I suggest a bit with a harsh curb—a Spanish bit, Mr. Ormonde."

A sound of singing came from the house. It swelled out upon them suddenly, as if the singer had just opened a door.

"She is coming," murmured Lorrimer. "Au revoir, Mr. Ormonde."

"Adieu," answered Creel, and to himself: "God be with me!"

The door of the house swung wide; in the dark arch stood Anne Berwick, and her song filled all the garden.

CHAPTER XV

DANGER

SHE WORE AN overcoat of a mouse-gray with the broad fur collar turned up about her face, and a tailored hat, one side flattened, sat at a slight, jaunty angle on her head as if it were already blown awry by the wind of swift driving.

Even in the darkness of the doorway Creel could see the flush of her cheeks and surmise the glimmer of her eyes and the last note of her song was framed like a smile upon her lips. She ran down the steps and came up to him with her hands outstretched. Lorrimer had paused and turned on his heel in the distance to watch the meeting, but she could not have been more open if they had been alone in the heart of a desert.

Her hands drew the arms of Creel about her and she swayed in toward him with uplifted face. Only for an instant; her lips barely brushed against his and before his arms settled about her she was away—as if a branch had been blown toward him and a dew-chilled leaf had touched his mouth and was swayed away by the wind again. There was no perfume about her, but a thrilling scent of freshness such as he had already breathed from the trees and the garden. About her—a fitting background!—was the sweetness of the opening blossoms.

He settled beside her in the roadster. The seat was deep and softly upholstered, circling half around him with a reassuring pressure; he could stretch his legs straight and leisurely, or jam them against the foot rest at will, there was so much room. All the while she hummed with a contented happiness, her eyes moist and bright as the morning. There was so much gladness in her that it kept her lips continually curved in an incipient smile and her glance kept in a wide embrace, Creel beside her and the swerve of the road before.

He watched her hand, ridiculously small and ineffectual in the gauntlet glove of rough, yellow leather. It settled on the emergency brake and released it; then he saw that the glove was plumped and filled with a soft strength. Her foot pressed out the clutch; the shoe was an absurdly tiny triangle on the roughened steel. He watched her try the brake and wondered where she would find the strength to control the lunging weight of that car once it was under way. Now the engine started with a soft purr, increased to a shrill whine; the clutch went in with imperceptible smoothness; the car moved down the driveway.

They gathered speed quickly as the big car nosed its way down the curves of the road, the gravel crunching with a rushing sound below them. In a moment they were straightening out for the gate; he saw the small foot which controlled the feed press down.

The machine did not lurch or jump ahead; it increased as smoothly as a well-muscled race horse who turns into the stream with a great reserve of strength still uncalled upon. But as the acceleration continued Creel felt the cushions press more closely on his shoulders and the wind cut sharply into his face; when he turned his head the trees at the side of the road were leaping into a blur behind him.

The broad wall at the gate caught up the rattle of the exhaust for an instant and flung the loud crackling into his ears. They were out of Windon Manor. There was now only the sharpening whine of the motor, the hum of the air on the windshield, the indescribable sound of wheels on the road.

They swung onto the main road with a lurch. Creel had caught hold on the door to prepare for the swerve, but in spite of that he was forced over against Anne. He was aware that she flashed up a puzzled glance at him; he set his teeth and glared straight ahead. They swept with a rising-hum up a hill and rushed down the further slope.

The fresh coolness of the morning had turned into a biting cold that sent a tingling in his nose and numbed his cheeks and mouth. He knew that his eyes were wide and staring; the knuckles of the hand that held onto the door were white with the strength of his grip and he knew that she was still sending curious, puzzled glances toward him now and again. Yet he could not for his life relax that grip. She raised a hand to her hat; his heart leaped into his throat and pounded there with sickening vigor.

Now the road lifted to meet a bridge. She gave a little cry of delight which the rush of wind clipped off short and sent whistling behind them, as if she had called out from a great distance. Down went the foot on the gas; the car leaped like a horse under the spur. Up the rise they rushed, seemed to lift bodily into the air, thudded in the center of the bridge, hurled down the further incline, met the road again with another jar, and swept up another and longer incline.

Now the road doubled around a hillside which dropped steeply down below them and in the heart of the valley beneath was a dense growth of trees tangled in the silver mist of the morning.

"Look!" cried the girl, and swept an ecstatic arm over the valley.

The car, as if about to follow her direction, lurched over to the side of the road; another foot and it would be down the slope. Creel cried out in inarticulate horror and clapped his hand across his eyes. Instantly the brakes screeched; they slowed down to a pace that allowed the blood to come burning into his cheeks and he turned to meet the terrified, wide gaze of Anne Berwick.

"What's wrong, Ed?" she pleaded. "What's happened? Is it your heart?"

"It's nothing," he answered stupidly. "Nothing at all."

She sighed with relief and the car accelerated, but slowly.

Then, with a keen suspicion she asked: "Ned, is there something wrong with my driving?"

Luckily at that instant a car hove in sight running in their direction and beyond it another machine which sped toward them, a large, red roadster.

"Ten dollars I can pass that machine before the roadster gets to it!" cried the girl gayly.

"Impossible!" groaned Creel, but he added hastily: "I mean, there's no point in trying that."

She had apparently heard only the first word. The engine hummed in a shrill crescendo and they rushed forward with breathless speed. Another bridge—they vaulted it like a hurdler. They lunged out on a sweeping curve, close behind the lead car, but with the roadster bearing swiftly down upon them.

"Not on the curve," shouted Creel. "Don't try to pass on the curve!"

But the scream of her siren drowned his voice and she looked up, as if in mockery of what he had said, with a gay assurance of success. At the sound of the siren the leading car had pulled over to the right of the road, but still it was far from the edge, and three cars, no matter how skillfully driven, could not possibly squeeze past on that boulevard; but now Anne was leaning over the wheel, the car sprang forward like a sentient thing answering a challenge.

She edged out, but fully a foot too short to give clearance, it seemed to Creel, and they rushed after the car ahead as if it were standing still. Yet the roadster was close, perilously close, and every second brought it yards closer.

Now they crept almost up to the car ahead of them; the siren shrieked again for more room, but there was no more room to give. Creel saw the driver to their right furiously jamming on the brakes. And the man in the roadster ahead was doing the same thing, rising up in his seat to get a stronger pressure. Yet still the roadster lunged at them with scarcely diminishing speed. Creel closed his eyes, tightened his grip on the door, and prepared for death.

Then an exhaust was crackling on either side, and above exhausts the shout of terrified voices—next a shrill cry of triumph from Anne. He opened his eyes and stared at her in a stupor; before them the road stretched, empty, and flashing under the light of the sun which had just pushed its rim above the mist of the morning.

"I'll wager I took the paint off his fender, eh?" she was calling. "Wasn't that a jolly close squeeze, Ned?"

Then the triumph died from her eyes and he knew that she was watching the deadly pallor of his face. It was as if she were looking into the most secret thoughts of his brain and reading him like a printed page. The hum of the motor dropped another octave. There was a moment of terrible silence during which she looked straight ahead down the gliding road.

At length: "Ned, tell me, man to man, are you, or are you not, in a blue funk?"

He could not have winced more sharply if she had struck him across the face with a whip and he knew that a dull and miserable red was rising in his face. It required every ounce of resolution in his mind and body to summon a sickly smile.

"Do I seem to be?"

"You do," she answered with instant and brutal frankness.

And she added, frowning: "If it were anybody but you, Ned Ormonde, I'd say you were frightened to death."

There was no use bluffing it out on that line he saw at once.

"To tell you the truth," he said quietly, "when you passed that car back there I thought I had come to the end of my rope."

She merely stared in mute wonder.

"But you—cars—Ned Ormonde—I thought—" she began in the wildest confusion, and could not finish her sentence.

"When there's another person at the wheel," said Creel, "I'm frankly miserable."

"Oh," she murmured slowly, with her doubt patent in her voice, "is that it? Then take the wheel yourself. I'm sure your driving won't bother me. I don't care a bit whether I'm doing it or some one else, you know. I'll stop the car and we'll change places if you wish."

But there rose in the mind of Creel a picture of Fifth Avenue traffic where they would soon be nosing their way among the snorting, purring hosts of automobiles; and in his small list of accomplishments the ability to drive a high-powered car was not included. And this machine of all others, tuned up to a point where it answered every touch like a living thing.

"Keep your place," said Creel with undue warmth, "but in the name of Heaven, Anne, have both hands on the wheel and don't *stand* on the gas."

SHOPPING WITH ANNE

SHE DROVE ON in a thoughtful silence, but though Creel knew perfectly of what she was thinking, it did not make him the happier; he was only grateful that her meditation made her drive more slowly. He understood that she was striving to co-ordinate a new impression of Edward Ormonde with her old idea of him. Edward Ormonde, daredevil, criminal for the sheer love of crime, and this man in the car beside her who had turned pale because she had chanced to brush close to another machine.

They were gliding over the high arch of the Blackwell's Island bridge before she spoke again. Under them was the glitter of East River, the pier heads piled with boxes and tarry barrels, to the left the strong, squat buildings of the island; and further to the left rose the Battery, still wrapped in its lower levels by that lingering morning mist, though its towers and spires and great blunt tops shouldered the fog aside and lunged far up into the white light.

It was too vast to have been built by man. It must have grown to music like the walls of Troy. As they sped closer to the roofs of the tenement houses on either side of the bridge Creel caught a refrain of that wonder-working music. Instead of the sharp twanging of the harp string he caught the jar of steel on steel, and in place of one singing voice there was the wide, sad murmur of the streets.

He turned to the girl. It was a poignant change from the universal to the particular. Was it not absurd that the face of a single girl, a face which he might enclose within the span of his finger tips, should have involved him in such a wretched tangle? A handful of beauty—what was that in the final sum of things? Ten years would undo her power, straighten the curve of her lips, dull her eyes, flatten her cheeks, wrinkle the purity of her throat.

And as for that wretched group of criminals at Windon Manor, he would simply board a train at the Grand Central Terminal, and within three days he would be out of sight and mind and back to the normal of life.

It was at this point that the girl spoke.

"Look!" she said, and pointing down the river toward Manhattan Bridge, she followed its arch with a curving gesture of her hand. That was all, a glance down the river, a gesture, a smile of happiness. But Creel forgot his reasoning and remembered only that she was lovely and the world was young. He felt the engine accelerate under the touch of her foot.

His heart began to beat rapidly. His mind was a machine and her voice was the touch that controlled it. Then he wanted to turn to her and say a host of foolish, tender things, but he checked himself. He knew that she could stop him with a single syllable. He was only an instrument, and she could play on him as she wished.

She had come over primarily to do some shopping, and they spent most of the day wandering from shop to shop down Fifth Avenue. The "madames" were extraordinarily attentive to Anne Berwick. If they did not know her it was patent at once that they wished to.

Creel watched her with a mingling of pride and awe. Her manner was perfect—neither condescending nor proud, but perfectly natural, perfectly direct. She was like a child, eager to find a beautiful toy and confident that one must be in each shop. For some reason the saleswomen talked to her with astonishing frankness. They told her all about their stock at once, and while they pointed out the good features of things she tried on, they were equally prompt to show her the deficiencies of material or style or workmanship, as if they were struggling to win a permanent patronage.

Her reasons for purchasing were equally mixed. She took a coat. It had an enormous collar of sables, and the bottom of the coat was deeply trimmed with the same rich fur. The price staggered Creel; but Anne took the coat neither because of price nor fur. She liked the line of the garment. And she was still talking about the way the collar could be turned up around the face as they reached the street. On the other hand she bought a hat of the flimsiest stuff and an odd design because the color would go well with one of her dresses.

The moment she was out of a shop and on the street her manner changed abruptly. At first it puzzled Creel and then amused him. Her eyes, usually so lighted by eagerness and traveling everywhere, now were fixed straight before her; her lips assumed a stony rigidity. He saw the reason for the change after a time. She was one of those who draw attention as flowers draw bees. Volleys of glances searched her as they passed by, but they slipped from her like water from stone; she was armed against observance.

Finally he asked frankly: "Why do you do it? What fun do you get from being pleasant to look at, Anne, if you pay no attention to admiration?"

She turned upon him eyes as chilly and unsearchable as the devotee's dream of Nirvana.

"Don't!" urged Creel. "It makes me feel like the vanishing point."

"Do you think I miss a single glance that comes my way?" she answered, with a sudden reversion to living warmth. "Why, Ned, it's like incense to me; I live on it as—as—"

She laid a hand on his arm and laughed at him.

"Don't you see it's all a game? If they knew I was watching they wouldn't look. When a girl is attractive the world is a stage and she is always behind the footlights playing to the audience, waiting for applause, but always pretending she doesn't hear a whisper or feel a glance."

"Anne," he broke out, "you're vain as the devil!"

He bit his lip as soon as he had spoken, but she slipped her arm through his, chuckling. For the first time since they left Windon Manor he felt that she was really close to him.

"I was wondering when you'd come to life, Ned. Of course I'm vain; and of course I'm glad you know it. I was afraid you'd be jealous. Do you know, I think of marriage as I think of jail!"

He could not answer. She went on contentedly, heedless of his expression:

"Chains on my feet—I couldn't walk where I want to. Chains on my eyes; I could only look at one face. And any one thing is apt to grow a bit monotonous, isn't it? I'm glad you're going to understand."

He stopped short, so that she swung around a little and partially faced him.

"Anne," he said steadily, looking into her eyes, "you take a most unconscionable lot for granted."

To his amazement she burst into prolonged, merry laughter; and one or two passers-by glanced at her and smiled in sympathy.

"Come along," she said at last, and drew him again down the pavement. She produced a handkerchief and dabbed at her eyes now and again, still laughing.

"Oh," she murmured, "you're going to be no end of fun."

He asked sternly: "Are you making a mock of me, Anne Berwick?"

"No. Edward Ormonde," she mimicked, "I'm not making a mock of you."

"I might as well tell you at once," he went on, "that I'm of a deucedly jealous temper."

He felt that he was being extremely stupid and flat in everything he said, but each syllable he spoke seemed to delight her more and more. She looked up at him now, her eyes lighted by happy curiosity.

"Are you going to watch me every minute?" she asked.

"Every second!"

"Like a *jailer?*"

"Exactly! You might as well know what to expect."

She made no answer, but he felt an increasing buoyancy in her step. Her arm rested less heavily in his; she seemed to be more aloof, more independent. Presently he heard her humming softly to herself.

"Anne!" he said sharply.

"Well?"

"You're a flirt by nature and by conscious cultivation."

"I'm sorry," murmured Anne.

"And it's got to be changed."

"I wish it could be changed."

"It will be."

He opened and closed his right hand masterfully.

He was suddenly aware of a tightening grip; she was almost hugging his arm into the soft, warm stuff of her coat.

"I didn't think it could be possible," she said. "It's too good to be true."

Open suspicion hardened his voice.

"What?"

"I'll tell you a profound secret. Lean down a bit so no one else will hear it!"

He obeyed, and heard: "Edward Ormonde is just like any other man!"

CHAPTER XVII

THE CONFESSION

IT WAS PATENT why she bore with his stupidity now. In Andrew Creel such talk as theirs had been would have bored her to extinction, but that Edward Ormonde, doubtless as famous for breaking hearts as for cracking safes, should be reduced to the level of common masculinity was a supertribute to the girl.

He proved this theory by a number of experiments during the rest of the day, and the more baldly commonplace his remarks were, the more the girl was delighted. Generalizations upon the world and life she greeted with the keenest enjoyment, and his silences she apparently valued more than his speech. She would hum to herself through one of the pauses and all the while watch him with a hidden train of thought passing swiftly behind her eyes.

It was one of these moments of observation that finally strained his endurance to the breaking point. They sat in the evening in a famous old French restaurant near the Battery. She had finished her salad, and now she sat with her elbows on the edge of the table, the agile white hands folded beneath her chin, steadied by one upright forefinger, and her eyes upon his face.

She watched him with as little embarrassment as a grown woman watches a child—watched until he felt as if there were a mask before his face—a veil of shadows that formed the features of Edward Ormonde. It was upon that mask that her eyes dwelt; it was the name of Edward Ormonde, repeated softly to herself, that made her lips tremble and then curve in the tenderest of smiles. It made Creel feel like a combination of sneak thief and eavesdropper.

He ground his teeth, and then, "Good chef here," he said.

She nodded, smiling more broadly, and a flush went up his face. He felt it burning on his cheeks and felt his forehead moist. Moreover, she was noting every detail with quiet enjoyment. Edward Ormonde was blushing like a self-conscious girl.

"Anne," he broke out, and he leaned, frowning, far across the table, "I have something to say to you."

She waited, her eyes half veiled, prepared for some absurdity:

"I am not Edward Ormonde!" said Creel.

She started, but not as he had intended. Her eyelashes raised and her glance centered hard upon him for an instant. Then the brilliant points of light softened and spread. She began to examine her finger nails, transparent and absurdly pink.

"Really?" murmured Anne Berwick.

"Look at me!" he commanded.

She obeyed, and he caught a staggering glimpse of amused assurance.

"Anne," he repeated with terrible gravity, "I am not Edward Ormonde."

"Oh dear!" cried Anne Berwick softly. "Then who in the world are you?"

"My name," he began, as one who starts a long narrative, "is Andrew Creel."

She went on, deepening her voice with marvelous accuracy to match his tone: "I was born in the little village of What-not, which nestles on the shore of Loch Lomond. At the time this story opens I was a sturdy young fellow of some eighteen years, strong, gay, innocent, loving nothing in the world so much as my Scottish heather. Ah, bright heather, and sweet hills of

Scotland, a since those innocent days how far I have roamed! And how many—"

"Anne!" he cut in, his lips compressed until they made only a thin white line.

"And then?" she asked brightly.

"Are you going to listen to me?"

"Of course I am."

His eye dared her. "My name is Andrew Creel."

He paused, but her lips, at least, did not interrupt.

"Chance and accident have thrown me into Windon Manor. I have no right to the position I hold there. I have not, and I never shall, carry the name of Edward Ormonde."

"What a terrible tangle everything is in," she remarked without the slightest emotion.

He persisted, determined to break through her mockery.

"If you ask me why I have not exposed my true identity to you before—"

"I don't ask, by no means!" murmured Anne Berwick.

"It was because, once in Windon Manor, I dared not expose myself for fear of my life, on the one hand, and because on the other hand I loved you, Anne, the moment I laid eyes on you."

She cried with mock tragedy: "But what shall we do, Andrew?"

"We'll stop laughing and become serious," he answered grimly.

"I'll do even that, if you wish."

"I'm not trying to excuse my conduct," went on Creel. "I only want you to know me as I am."

"Thank you," said Anne faintly.

"You may despise me after I have told the whole story. But I had rather have you despise me as Andrew Creel than love me under a name which is not mine."

Suddenly her hand dropped over his. She was laughing.

"Ned Ormonde, you foolish, delightful fellow," she said, "do you want me to say that I'll care for you just as much, no matter what you are or have been? I'll say it if you wish."

What could he do? He stared at her in baffled rage.

"Oh, Ned," she said at last, laughing again, "you real boy—you eternal child—I wouldn't love you half so well if you were as clever and intriguing and brilliant—and—and—hard, as you usually are!"

In turn she leaned toward him, confiding, and he had not the breath to interrupt her. "Don't you suppose that I know about you? I do! All the way from Lady Winderley to that girl of the Comedy. And I'm so glad—so *glad!*—that you're not confident and careless with me. I never thought—honestly!— that I'd ever be so flattered by seriousness in a man."

"Anne," he said, "I feel like—"

"Well?"

"I feel like spanking you!"

"Because I don't believe that silly tale? Well, I will believe it, if you want. Go ahead, Ned—Andrew, I mean—and I won't interrupt a single time."

"I shall not," he decided. "But when you learn the truth, later on, as you're bound to, remember to-night."

"Of course I shall."

"And you won't blame me?"

"Not the least bit."

It was quite hopeless to go on. Moreover, his head was spinning; he hardly knew whether or not he wanted her to know the truth. Then, as he sat with his head bowed, he heard her cry out softly, and he looked up to see her glancing past him with eyes of fire.

She was so changed that he could hardly realize that it was the same girl who faced him, no more than the tabby cat curled by the hearth and blinking at the fire is the same swift creature which stalks the bird in the bush.

CHAPTER XVIII

THE THEFT

"HAVE YOU HAD enough to keep you from being hungry before we get home to Windon Manor?" she asked, her eyes still fixed on some distant object.

"Yes."

"Then get the check and pay the bill and be ready to start. We may have marching orders any moment."

"What's up?"

"A game."

"Well?"

"Wait. She's caught my eye. If you turn now she'll know that we're talking about her. Here comes our waiter. Turn and beckon him, and when you do it, look three tables back and one row to the left."

He turned obediently and summoned the waiter. Three tables back and one row to the left he saw a man and a woman—a strange pair to have caught the eye of Anne Berwick and set such a fire in it. For they were broad people with tanned faces and the red of good health shining through the skin. Newly rich, undoubtedly. She wore a very low-necked dress of some black, fluffy stuff; and she had a much befeathered hat with a transparent brim. As for the man, he bulged uneasily in his tuxedo.

"Did you see it?" asked Anne eagerly.

He studied her in amazement. Her nostrils quivered. She sat

99

more erect and lightly poised in her seat; one hand on the edge of the table was clenched hard.

"See what? Two over-rich, underdressed people?"

"No, no! *It!* At her throat!"

He turned and flashed back another glance. On the broad expanse of the woman's breast there was a glimmer and then a flash of green. Her breast stirred; a thousand green lightnings flashed against his eyes. He turned back to Anne, breathing hard.

"What a jewel! By Jove, what an emerald! But what's the matter with you. Anne?"

"It will go perfectly," she said, narrowing her eyes in criticism, "with that yellowish dress of mine."

The waiter had come with his change and he picked it up automatically. Slowly it was penetrating his thoughts that Anne Berwick was going to steal that emerald pendant.

He said at length:

"It won't do, Anne."

"What?"

"You can't take a toy from a child; and that fat, lumbering ox of a woman is just as helpless as a child."

"Ah, but there is Gastre of the force at that little table in the corner. See! He has his eye on them every minute."

"Gastre?"

"He's an old bloodhound; it's a hard trail that fools Gastre, I'll tell you. But think of plucking the apple under his eyes. See him there combing his little white beard and looking at nothing. Bah! I know him too well. He is seeing everything and every face in this room and he would be able to sketch the hundred faces one by one in case of need. That's Gastre. Haven't you heard of him?"

"I think I have, but I can't place him."

"Or," she went on, inspired, "I might commission you to get it for me! Ned, I would give a year of life to watch you work."

"Watch *me?*" he stammered.

She looked at him with some anger.

"Ned," she cried at length, "I wish you would wake up and be yourself!"

Then she added swiftly: "But if I have to I'll get it myself."

"Anne—" he began, panic-stricken.

"Quick!" she urged. "They're getting up—he's helping her on with her things. Get me into my coat, Ned! We've got to reach that door on their heels!"

He protested, but his stammerings meant nothing. She was already on her feet; and his brain was whirling so rapidly that he could only mutely help her into the coat. While he was struggling into his own coat she was already starting toward the door.

He regained her side with a few long, swift paces, a protest—a command, prepared on his lips, but she cut in: "We hurried too fast. Old Gastre is already watching me. Ned, I wouldn't miss this moment for a year of life. Do something, laugh—talk—swear—anything so that I can seem wrapped up in the noise you make."

It was not hard to laugh. The whole situation was such a ridiculous mixture of the comic and the tragic that he laughed heartily. She joined him at once with the lightest mirth. Then, under her breath: "Good! Gastre is going through the door first! Now, Ned!"

"In the name of Heaven, Anne!" he murmured fervently. "Don't do it!"

But she laughed back over her shoulder as they reached the door. He would never forget her as she looked that moment, tilting back, her face flushed, twin devils in her eyes. The prey was before her, bulkier than ever in their wraps, and their loud voices boomed before and behind. Creel reached for the arm of Anne to hold her back by main force, but she had already slipped through behind the others; he could only join her in the street.

"Well?" he asked breathlessly.

But instead of answering she went straight to the automobile. The engine was purring when he settled clown beside her, and they nosed their way up the street at once.

A shiver of relief passed down the spine of Creel, and finally he remarked with a real gayety: "You hadn't figured on that fur collar of her coat, Anne, eh?"

She turned full about in the machine and stared at him in frank amazement.

"Good Heavens, Ned!" she cried. "Did you think *that* would stop me?"

"Do you mean to say—" he began, and the color sank from his face.

"That I have it?"

She laughed in low content.

"Look!"

Before his eyes dangled the jewel on its chain of gold.

"Would the fur collar have stopped even the great Ormonde?" she continued triumphantly. "Why, that was what made my game safe!"

"You—we—will never get away from Gastre," answered Creel, and he shook his head gloomily. "He watched us coming toward the door; you yourself admitted that he never forgot faces."

"But the fur collar," said the girl. "Don't you see how that saves us? She'll never think about the safety of the pendant until she takes off her coat again. And then—they'll probably be at home—they'll figure that the chain must have broken and start searching the pavements all the way home from the restaurant. Ha, ha, ha! I can see those two fat old people straining their eyes by lantern light and dodging through the traffic. Oh, Ned Ormonde!"

He protested miserably. "But you can never wear it. Every one in America will know it."

"I can wear it at home, for you," she suggested.

"For me?" He choked.

"And when we get to Paris."

"Anne, you'll torture me. Every time a man looks sharply at you I'll be sure he'd recognized the pendant!"

She was silent. They were passing through a dark side street and he could only make out the outline of her face as she turned again toward him.

"Tell me in one word," she said dryly, "what you want me to do with it? Pack it in gauze and look at it once a year?"

"Return it to the police."

This drew an inarticulate gasp from her.

"Don't you see?" he explained bitterly. "Every time I look at you and see that pendant I'll remember that it belongs—"

"To another woman with a fat neck?" she asked, smiling.

"Perhaps. But the thought of it makes me sick, Anne, and—"

She burst out in a sudden fury. "Ormonde, you are either—mad—or else the most profound hypocrite that ever breathed. The pendant? I don't care whether or not I ever set my eyes on it again. Take it, and do what you want with it. I'm through!"

And she tossed the jewel into his lap.

Among other things she was through talking. She spoke not a single word throughout the remainder of the ride, and he sat miserably clenching the hard stone against the palm of his hand. He knew that he was very near indeed to the end of his rope.

CHAPTER XIX

ADVICE FOR ANNE

AND SO STRONG was that cold, sick feeling in the pit of his stomach that he paid no heed to her driving on the way home—and she literally drove like a storm wind. After they had run the machine into the garage she left him at the door of the house. He made one futile effort to detain her and to explain; he touched her arm carefully and asked her to wait a moment.

They stood in the big, dimly lighted hall, and she turned to him a face flushed with anger and graven with pain. There was no bitter feminine subtlety about her. She took both his hands and studied him with a fierce interest.

"Ned Ormonde," she said, "you aren't what I thought you'd be. I'm puzzled. I don't know what to make of things. And I think it would be a lot wiser if we were to be strangers to each other for a few days. Good night!"

She whirled away from him and went straight up to the rooms of James Ashe. For a long time she had been in the habit of going to Ashe for advice when she was in trouble; she went to him instinctively now.

The body servant of Ashe met her at the door. He was an Afghan whom Ashe had picked up in his travels, probably in one of those grisly adventures of which Ashe never spoke to living man. He was one of those very old men from whom the blood seems to have been dried up; he was withered and warped by the long passage of years into a crooked frame of big bones and flaps of skin.

In his day he must have been a fine, strong fellow, as wild as any Afghan youth that ever wielded a knife; where the tiger had clawed him two dirty white lines ran from his temple to his jaw, and he still possessed speed of hand and eye and would possess it until he died or withered quite away. He wore his white turban, as usual when he was in the house, and had his legs wrapped up to the knees in narrow, white bandages. The rest of his costume was more or less occidental.

It was this skull-like face which met Anne Berwick at the door and she stared with awe into the black hollows of his eyes. He bowed her in and closed the door behind her. A singularly fitting servant for such a man as Ashe. As she felt toward the servant so she felt, very nearly, toward the master. He was different.

She saw him now reclining in a low ottoman piled deep with cushions, a black silk cap upon his head, and wearing a dressing gown of some thick white stuff. He looked like some captain of industry who has cleft his way to the van by dint of brutal force; but he lived like a Sybarite. He loved the silken touch with a consuming passion, but he admitted nothing which might disturb the strength of his mind. He neither drank nor smoked; he had never been known to gamble.

Sometimes she thought she could have liked him better if he had possessed some of these weaknesses. His armor was too complete: there were no fissures in it through which the weapons of the ordinary man could reach him. With her he had always unbent, but even Anne felt that she could never truly know him. His presence fell about her like a shadow of eternal dimness. He terrified her and such terror is only a step from love. She knew to what it might lead and that doubled her fear of him.

James Ashe stood up to receive her.

"Lie down here," he advised. "You are very tired."

She had almost accepted when she turned on him with a sharp question: "How do you guess that?"

"You're generally tired when you come to see me," said Ashe, and his calm, imperturbable eyes surveyed her coolly from head to foot. "I've been waiting for you a long time. Will you rest here?"

But instead she sat down among the cushions of the ottoman and regarded him almost sternly, almost defiantly. He drew up a chair just opposite and sat down with his hands resting passively on his knees. He was as impenetrable as an image of Buddha.

"I'm beaten," she broke out suddenly. "I don't know where I stand."

He made no answer. Sometimes his silences made her yearn to shake him like a sullen boy.

"So I've come to you for help," she went on.

"Will you have some black coffee first?" he asked. "Thick, black, Turkish coffee?"

"Will you have a cup with me?" she queried.

"I never drink it," said Ashe.

"Then I'll do without it."

"You are angry," he announced calmly.

"Because you have no weaknesses. You're too invincible. You leave no openings."

"Anne, if you knew how many weaknesses I have you'd despise me."

"Name some of them."

"You already know the greatest one."

She colored and then waved the subject aside.

"But I've come to talk about myself. Will you help me?"

He did not speak. But his silences could mean "yes "or "no" as well as the spoken words of most men.

"It's Ormonde, of course," she said at last, and waited with her eyes fixed upon his face. The pause endured for a full ten seconds. Then his lips twitched very slightly into something that was not a smile, and his eyes wavered from hers the slightest trifle.

"You hate him with your whole heart, don't you?" she asked curiously. "Well, that gives me heart to go on talking. Because I think I'm on the verge of hating him, also."

He moistened his compressed lips and his eyes came back to hers.

"That pleases you, doesn't it? Well, it's all strange and mixed up. When I first met Ormonde in the garden I—loved him, Jimmy!"

She watched him wince and change color; it was one of the two or three times in her life that she had seen him evince such a palpable emotion. One other time—but she shuddered even remembering it.

She went on hurriedly: "I know you don't want to hear this, but I have to explain. When I first met him he was everything I expected him to be. I felt his force even when he was silent; I knew the sharpness of his mind; I knew his courage and his experience. He was in our danger, but he never changed color to the very last. And I knew he was the one man in the world I was ready to follow. Do you see?"

He nodded slowly.

"Then I went out with him to-day. It was partly funny and it was partly horrible. You know how much we've heard about his daredeviltry with an automobile—and particularly that drive from Glasgow to Woolwich? Well, I sped up a bit in the roadster—mind you, I didn't turn it loose—and Edward Ormonde—the great Edward Ormonde—hung onto the side of the car like a scared girl taking her first ride.

"Well, at first I thought that something might be wrong with him. Sick, perhaps. I slowed down and asked if he was ill, but he said nothing.

"Later on we ran between two machines. Pretty tight squeeze, but we must have had a couple of inches at least on each side.

Jimmy, the great Edward Ormonde closed his eyes and turned the color of a dying man—a sort of ratty white. Ugh!"

She shuddered at the memory.

"But I made up my mind that I'd not jump to conclusions. Till this evening, when we were dining, he made another queer move. I saw a fine emerald with old Gastre standing guard over it like a watchdog. Fine trick to take it under the nose of Gastre, I said to myself, and going behind them into the street I took it from under a big fur collar.

"Well, Jimmy, when we started home, and Ormonde found out that I had the thing with him he acted as if—as if—"

"As if he were horrified?" filled in James Ashe quietly.

"How did you guess that?" she challenged.

"Listen to me!" said the big man, and he leaned his massive shoulders closer to her. "I could guess a great many other odd things about this—Ormonde."

"Why do you speak of him like that? Jimmy, don't make me think it's jealousy!"

"It isn't," he assured her. "Upon my honor it isn't jealousy. It's true that he stands in my way, this—Ormonde—and after a time I shall brush him out of my path. In the meantime, Anne, take my solemn word that if you consider this fellow too seriously, you'll spend the rest of your life laughing at yourself because you've done it. Will you believe me?"

"Just what do you know?"

"Some day I'll tell you—unless you find out for yourself. Now tell me frankly, man to man: if you didn't know this fellow to be the famous Edward Ormonde, how would you judge him by to-day?"

"I have to put it in slang," she said. "I'd call him a plain—boob!"

"Well," murmured James Ashe, "try to forget that he's Edward Ormond and watch him for three days as if he were simply an ordinary man. I think you'll find the results interesting."

CHAPTER XX

THE END OF THE ROPE

IN HIS ROOM Creel sat down to the hardest thinking he had ever done in his life. He had always been a logical man, and in this crisis he was more supremely logical than ever before.

He admitted frankly that he was wholeheartedly in love with Anne Berwick. The thought of her would not leave him. It stayed at his side. As he sat now at the table he felt her as if she were behind his chair, or outside the door with her white hand on the knob and about to enter.

But he knew definitely that he had lost her. He conducted a brief review of their relations. At that first meeting in the garden she had loved him, he knew, as deeply as he loved her; but it was not Creel she had seen—it was the mysterious spirit of Edward Ormonde that had taken possession of him. It was that same spirit which enabled him to chain her to him, to solve the problem of Robert Lorrimer and the old miser, and in the end to conquer even James Ashe in the twilight of the garden.

It was James Ashe who had won her; and it was Andrew Creel who had lost her. For the spirit of Ormonde had deserted him after that first time of need. He could not explain it. He only knew that for a time he had been transfigured, another self. And now the wild spirit of adventure was flown from him and he was again Andrew Creel, the listless, the ennuied.

One day had sufficed to show him to her in part. Another day or so would be sufficient to tear from him whatever veils of romantic interest he still retained in her eyes. Should he stay here, then, until the last fictitious garment was torn from him and he stood like a scarecrow naked to the mockery of Anne Berwick? Ah, the keen, merciless laughter of Anne! She would pillory him forever!

No, it would be far better to leave Windon Manor at once and forever. His oaths to the society still held him, but he had good reason to feel that Ashe would be quite willing to dissolve those oaths and let him go—the farther away the better. And as for the girl—it might be that when he was at a distance she would revert to her dreams of him—her dreams of an Edward Ormonde who wore the face of Andrew Creel.

It took a long struggle before he reached this point in his resolutions; then he rose and went straight to Ashe.

He found the leader of the society alone; but he was pacing the floor in silent excitement, for Anne Berwick had left him hardly five minutes before. To that calm, expressive face he related his purpose shortly.

"I have come to confess defeat. Mr. Ashe," he said, "and you'll admit that I've come to the quarter where it's hardest to confess it. Ashe, I'm beaten. I have given up my hopes. The girl sees through me. I surrender any claims to her."

Ashe yawned prodigiously, but his eyes glittered with a steady malice. "So far," he murmured, "so good."

Creel kept his voice calm. "I've decided to leave. But first I'll have to have you, Mr. Ashe, dissolve the oaths which keep me here. I've an idea that you'll be glad to have me go," he added bitterly.

"In time," nodded Ashe. "The day will come when I shall, perhaps, be glad to have you go; but that day has not yet come."

"Just what do you mean by that?"

"My dear Mr. Creel," said the big-shouldered man, "you have, as you say, lost. You are defeated. However, you are not yet routed." His voice deepened and increased in volume. "You have not suffered as I have suffered, but I am going to keep you here until you see Anne Berwick scorn you openly, before all men. When that time comes, sir, you will be free to go. Until that time, there is not money enough in the world to buy your ransom. Do you understand?"

"It is quite clear," murmured Creel miserably.

He felt no resentment, properly so called. He was only gloomily aware that what Ashe said was the truth.

"And after the score of Anne is settled," went on Ashe grimly, "there will still remain the affair of the Bigbee case. We shall have to strive to come to terms on that, Mr. Creel."

Creel lifted his fallen head.

"I'm not going to threaten you," he said, "but I wish to suggest that you're following a dangerous course, Ashe. Once before, to put it baldly, you found me too strong for you. Doesn't it occur to you that the time may perhaps come when I'll be again too strong for you?"

"All things," replied the other, "are possible. I have no desire to follow the sure thing."

"But think again," urged Creel. "You have me now admitting that I've lost. You can make a contract with me in which you are everywhere the complete gainer except that a certain deep malice will be unassuaged. Sacrifice your revenge, Ashe, to your common sense. In the morning I may repent the bargain I am willing to make now. In the morning I may be another man."

"What?" cried Ashe under his breath, drawing back a pace. "Another man?"

"Edward Ormonde, in fact," replied Creel.

"Bah!" sneered the other. "I've heard this fool's talk before. And even if you were Ormonde in flesh and blood, I would defy you still, Creel, and keep you here for the death grapple."

There was no appeal from that decision. Creel saw and admitted the last defeat. He turned on his heel and went back to his own room.

There he turned out the lights and sat with head bowed. It is a bitter thing to admit the superior strength of another man, and the force of James Ashe was like a leaden weight upon his spirit. He had met his master, and between the upper millstone of Ashe and the nether stone of Anne he would be ground to a shameful dust. So he sat in the dark. He dared not keep on the light, lest he should see his own reflection in the glass and be forced to observe his own staring eyes, wide with fear.

Outside a rising wind moaned about the house, a dreary and congenial note. But by degrees, sharpening in tone, it caught his fancy. It was too weird a music to take entirely into his despondent mood. There was more of the suggestion of battle and struggle in it. It cut into the ears like wind-blown battle cries. And finally it filled Creel with a vague restlessness, a discontent with the dark.

He began to forget his own problems. He felt a strong and increasing desire, to be out under the stars with that wind in his face. That wind in his face! The very thought made his heart leap. He rose; he flung up the sash of the window; he let the full gale beat in upon his face.

It carried a mist that made his hair and eyebrows wet at once. It whipped against his skin; it rattled some papers in the room behind him, and it drummed a loose picture against the wall. Aye, there was an ecstasy in it, a force and a wildness. He thought of wanderers leaning against that wind this night. He thought of the gallant schooner staggering up from the trough and tossed on the dizzy top of the groundswell. He thought of far lands and distant temples scourged by this wind. He saw the coconuts shaken from the palm tops. He saw the sandstorm, dense as night, overwhelm the caravan. He saw the terrible arctic snows filling earth and heaven with a wild uproar.

And out of the pictures rose a keen sense of power, as if it were his hand which had stirred up the sand and tossed down the snow and shaken the lofty top of the palm. Yes, there was a sense of kinship—or at least the welcome presence of a familiar thing.

He tore open his shirt at the throat; he bent back his head.

The mists parted far above him. He saw for an instant a terrific vista into a dim world of stars. The voice of the wind rose now like singing from his own throat. It lifted his spirit upon its own viewless wings. Finally a sharp gust of rain rattled against the panes of the window and warned him to draw the sash down.

He turned back into the room; he reached automatically for the light and switched it on, and as he did so he saw his face in the mirror—his hair on end, his coat wet and shining, his lips somewhere between a smile and silent laughter, and a nameless fire in his eyes.

He remembered then, suddenly, that a moment before he had been afraid, defeated, broken. He laughed aloud.

The wind had led him first to Edward Ormonde on the prow of the ship with the murmur of the bow wave beneath: the wind had blown back to him once more the same wild spirit.

An ineffable happiness filled him. That night he did not sleep.

CHAPTER XXI

WIND

HE DID NOT sleep. He slipped into a raincoat and went down to the garden and walked for a long time aimlessly to and fro. Now and again the storm shook drenching showers from the trees above him, roaring at his ears. Again it walked far off with a sound of distant roaring through the tree tops.

A scent of exquisite freshness rose from the garden mold, and between the rattling of the showers Creel could hear the crinkling of the ground as it drank the water. It filled him with a sense of eternal order, the eternal goodness of the things of earth. Out of mud and water grows the rose and the pine tree; out of the empty wind came the spirit of Edward Ormonde, transforming him.

Yet he made some plans as he walked there in the thick dark. The strength that was with him might be gone in a moment, and he knew that he must use the power which had come to him again so mysteriously this night to gain Anne definitely for his own and to break away from the society.

It was then that he drew his inspiration. He conceived the plan of out-Heroding Herod, of outroaring the wind, of breaking out with a series of crimes so wildly and foolishly bold that even the society would count itself fortunate to be done with him, maugre the cost, and Anne, if she cared for him, would beg him on her knees to give up that reckless and headlong course of crime.

Sleep? He could not sleep for the sheer joy of it. He had no need of sleep. The wind fell long before morning. The stars came out, first one by one and then a sudden down-looking of the hosts so near and bright that he felt the curve of the earth's surface pressing him up closer and closer to the heavens.

When the first rosy hand of the dawn put out above the eastern hills he went back to his room, bathed, changed, and sauntered down through the house while still there was hardly a sound of life. Only a few servants were cleaning in the hall and washing down the steps upon which the storm had thrown up a scattering of sand and mud. So he went out again into the garden to walk there until breakfast should be ready. He was ravenously hungry. He could have eaten heartily of dry bread and drunk cold water with the relish of the richest wine. But there was no accompanying sign of weakness.

His hunger was that of the athlete prepared for the contest— all lean muscle and ready brawn—or the wolf coursing his prey. He began to whistle. He did not know where the tune came from. It sprang ready made into his brain, but it expressed to him all the gladness of the morning. Now the sun pushed up. No gradual change from night to day. There was one blinding flash of light from the wet leaves and along the windows of the manor house.

"Anne should be here," he said to himself, and even as he said it he heard the front door of the house close and, turning, he saw Anne Berwick standing on the front steps. He stepped out toward her.

She wore a house dress, something of a thin and soft material with a color between rose and lavender. The dress billowed about her and clung when the breeze blew steadily. It made her seem marvelously light and very young and slender. At sight of him she had drawn herself up and some of the light died out of her face.

"I heard some one whistling," she said coldly, as he drew nearer, and she was about to turn back into the house.

"Well?" he queried.

"I thought it might have been Mr. Ashe," she continued in the same tone.

"Ashe?" he replied lightly. "Go up and rout him out of bed, Anne. He's sleeping. The morning wouldn't waste itself on such a dullard."

She measured him with a glance of some contempt and some indifference; but there was a puzzled light behind her eyes. Then she turned as if she were about to follow his suggestion.

"But on second thought," said Creel, "I guess you'd better stay out here with me."

She was both dry and definite. "I have something to do within the house," she said. "I can't waste my time out here in the garden."

"Tut, tut," he answered; "you are too young to be so dull."

And with that he possessed himself of her arm. The act took his breath in a measure. He was shocked at the boldness of Andrew Creel. He felt as if a second self were standing by and gaping at such rude self-confidence. He was drawing her down the garden path.

"The sun on the tree; the light on the windows; the wetness of the ground—look at that bedraggled caterpillar crawling up the rosebush—these are things for you to see, Anne. Stay out here with me." He drew her on.

But she brought them to an abrupt halt. "I really don't wish to walk just now," she said icily.

"But I do," answered Creel with incredible insolence, "and I wish it enough to make up for indifference."

"Mr. Ormonde!" she said sharply.

"Come, save your dignity," he answered—"save it for an audience. Now there's not a living thing to enjoy it except the birds in the trees. Listen to them—gay little beggars! Come along, Anne, you know in your heart of hearts you're wild to."

She hesitated between anger and alarm. "Were you drinking last night?" she asked sharply.

He loosened her arm and looked her over with a frank disgust.

"You're right," he said. "Go back to the house. If you stay out here you'll be spoiling my morning for me."

She flushed under his look, and then her glance steadied and brightened. "What in the world has happened to you, Ned?"

"The morning, in the first place," he said, "and you in the second and a desire for action in the third."

"What sort of action?"

They were wandering under the trees now;

"Any kind. I'm tired of the stupid life here at Windon Manor. Good God, do you people do nothing but sit about and yawn your lives away."

"Yawn—our—lives—away!" she cried, amazed.

"Exactly. Action—that's the thing—action. Every moment wasted sitting still or standing still is a moment lost forever. Here we are this instant. What are we doing?"

"What could we do?"

"Make love to one another. Why not?"

"Ned!" she cried; but her reproof was not altogether serious. "If you want to talk, why not chatter away about the morning?"

"I can see it well enough in your face," he answered gayly. "The rose of it in your cheeks, the light of it in your eyes—"

"Nonsense!"

But she was laughing now.

"The wind of it in your breath," he went on, "the perfume in your hair, the delight on your lips!"

He gathered her in his arms, bent back her head with a rude force," lowered his lips almost to hers, and then stepped back and loosed her with such suddenness that she staggered and almost fell.

"If you pluck the rose, it withers," said Creel. "It loses its perfume. It becomes a dead thing in a day. And if you're to be lovely all your life, you must be untouched and unused. Have you ever thought of that?"

She was panting, excited, bewildered.

"I can't follow what you mean," she stammered.

"You don't have to. Just be happy, Anne. Look up! So! Let the light of the morning strike you. In a light such as this you are positively beautiful, Anne! Action, action, action—that's the thing we want! How'll we strike into the fresh heart of this dawn? How shall we, Anne?"

"Whatever you say," she answered, carried away by his random eloquence.

"The car—and I shall drive," he added significantly.

He knew perfectly well that it was to court destruction to ride in that high-powered roadster this morning; but there was one picture which he had to wipe out of her mind this morning, and that was the sight of Andrew Creel clinging desperately to the door of the car, with set and staring eyes of horror. Somehow he knew he'd be different this morning.

"Yes, yes," she agreed. "The car's the thing."

They had it out quickly, new washed and shining like a red jewel. Creel took his place at the wheel, and she slipped in beside him. He fumbled the gears; they were familiar enough. At least he knew the general details of the mechanism. He started the motor and raced it to warm it up. The humming rose in a fierce crescendo. The big body quivered and trembled under him as if in fear—fear of him!

"We're off!" he shouted. "Hold on, Anne!"

CHAPTER XXII

SPEED

FEAR? FEAR OF speed? No sooner had the car started—not smoothly as under the touch of Anne's experienced hand, but with a jarring lurch—than Creel wanted wings—wings to break from the earth and hurtle through that bright eastern color into the very heart of the freshness of the morning. Fear?

He stepped on the gas—the car sprang out like a wild mustang with the blindfold removed from its eyes. Fear?

The roadster darted down the twisting driveway. It swept around a curve. The rear tires skidded on the wet gravel with a screech. It straightened out with spinning wheels. It clipped a corner of the road before Creel could turn it again and smashed a border of flowers, it careened with gathering speed further down the drive, it skidded again and demolished a whole hedge of roses.

"Ned!" came a startled cry at his side.

He knew from the sound rather than from actual sight that she was clinging to the side of the car, her face white and her eyes wide. Brutal joy swept through him, he felt as if his arms were around her, crushing her. They spun past a tree, raking off the bark with a rear fender, and then the car straightened out on the open road.

Now the paved road. It was smooth, clear. No travelers at this early hour, but it was still wet and shining with dazzling brilliance from the rain of the night before. Pools had gathered in slight depressions and the wheels scattered the water and sent it back in a fine, stinging mist. He had not the steady hand of the practiced driver, but had to keep working the wheel back and forth to keep the car in the road as they flew forward, leaving a snake's trail behind them. And at every twist, almost, there was an ominous skidding.

Through the gates of Windon Manor they caromed, with the roar of the exhaust barking at them. He threw it open. At once it crackled like musketry behind them. It was an alarm to be heard for miles through the placid heart of that shining morning.

They struck the main road, and he swung onto it with a sickening lurch.

They took a sharp bend on two wheels, and then he felt something warm pressing against his shoulder. He looked down. She was crouching far back in the seat, her thin dress fluttering about her face, and with that rosy color blowing about it, her skin was whiter than the white bell of the lily, her eyes were marvelously wide and dark. He wanted to swing her closer to him with his right arm. No, it was better to watch her from time to time, cringing, terrified, but ashamed to beg for less speed.

Fear? He stepped on the gas and pressed the lever clear down to the floor of the car. The roar of the exhaust was like the opening of a battery of rapid fire cannon!

Aye, they were flying now. At every rise of the ground the car seemed to leave the road and hurtle through the air. He could not keep it steady in the center. It would have almost baffled a skilled racer to have done that, and Creel merely caromed wildly from side to side, lurching, skidding terribly. The water that flew back at them misted the wind shield. He did not care. No matter how he drove, some exterior power would bring them safely back, or if they did not come safely back, what mattered it still? All men must die. Why not die in such a moment of perfect happiness?

He began to sing. Why not? A flock of birds swept close overhead flying in the same direction, but the car outstripped them! He waved an arm up to them and shouted a greeting.

That road to the left made a long detour through the hills. He would take that because it ran in a circle and ended again in front of Windon Manor. He had heard Robert Lorrimer say that.

But it was an uneven road. They crossed a hundred little ravines, small culverts, and at each of these the machine lifted from the first incline and seemed springing up toward the sky. The gas was open now, almost every inch of the way. The car lurched and wrenched and twisted.

Now an upgrade lowered the speed quickly. Then Creel was conscious that the girl had straightened a little beside him, though she still clung with a desperate energy to the side of the car. Her face was tilting up. She was staring, mutely imploring, into his eyes. But he would not turn.

Then she called. Her voice came as from a great distance through the rush of the exhaust. He turned to her now with a gesture, as if he had not heard her calling, begging him to go more slowly. And into the terror of her eyes he shouted:

"Anne, are you happy? Are you gloriously happy? The world is ours!"

They topped the rise. They sprang forward again with the terrible speed of old and he knew that she had slumped back once more in the seat. The warmth was again at his shoulder. Then something small and strong closed on his upper arm. It was her white hand, clinging to him instead of to the side of the car.

Still he would not relent. The brutal delight had him by the throat. The same death that threatened her threatened him, but he did not care. He was establishing a mastery which she would never question, though she lived to be a hundred.

What drove that car so fearlessly? Was it the body of Andrew Creel and the spirit of Ormonde?

Again it made no difference, save that the air sang past his ear and cut his face and all the glory of wanton speed was his.

Now she was pleading again as they lurched down an incline with terrific velocity.

"Ned!"

"Aye?" he called back.

They had to shout to make themselves heard.

"Slow up!"

"I can't."

A scream of horror replied.

"Ned, what's wrong with the car?"

"Not the car. Something's wrong with me."

"For God's sake!" she shrilled.

"I can't help it. I've got to travel."

A breathless curve made her wince back and clasp a thin hand across her eyes.

And his voice rang down at her as they rocked back on all four wheels again.

"Do you love me?"

"You'll kill us both!" she begged.

"Do you love me?" he repeated, and let the car shriek down a long descent with the engine at top speed.

"Yes," she screamed in mortal agony. "Yes, yes! Anything! But drive more slowly!"

"One minute more of speed!" he begged in turn. "I can't slow down!"

"You're mad, Ned! You're mad! You're throwing us both away!"

"What difference? Do you know a better way to die?"

"Ned!"

"Had you rather die with another man? Answer!"

But something of his madness seemed to take fire in her. He saw it flaming in her eyes.

"Let it go! Wide open, then!"

She threw her arms up, but the swerve of the car almost threw her out, and then rocked her back with jarring violence against him.

"Ten seconds to live a lifetime in. Do you care, Anne?"

"No, no, no!"

It was the wildest hysteria; he could see that. In another moment she might collapse. But now for a brief instant she shared all his own wild delight. They were joined, perfectly, in this insane abandon, rushing on toward nothingness. They leaped up a hill, they dived into a valley, they lunged around a bend.

Then hurtling down another gradual fall they darted around a bend at the very end of the descent. Blind madness seized him. One hand of iron gripped the wheel and steadied it in some futile measure. The other arm literally picked her up and crushed her against him. The white face lay on his shoulder; the transfigured eyes blazed against his own. He kissed her.

The blast of the wind forced a perfume from her hair and into his very soul; and something like an electric spark leaped from one to the other, numbing him. Under them the machine pitched like a ship on a stormy sea. He gave no heed to it; he did not glance at the road.

In another instant they would leap into nothingness; but they would perish, fused, made one for eternity.

She relaxed. Her head fell back. Her eyes were closed. Her beauty was the incredible loveliness of death. The car struck the rise to a bridge, lifted into the air, and with the thudding fall on the center of the bridge he looked back to the road again.

God or the devil or the ghost of Edward Ormonde at the wheel had kept them safe; through that long moment of blind ecstasy some other power had guided the car.

He released the gas lever. The rush of wind fell away from his face. His head nodded forward a little and he realized that he had been bracing himself with a strong effort against that terrific current of air. A warmth came back to him from the hot engine, and so, slowly, smoothly, they rolled through the gate of Windon Manor.

Before the garage one of the servants came out and seeing the limp body of Anne he cried out in alarm.

Other people appeared. Some one shouted from the house. Lorrimer and big-shouldered James Ashe were running toward them.

But Creel climbed from his seat, passed around the car, and brushed aside the reaching arms. He himself gathered up the inert body of Anne Berwick.

"What in the name of God has happened?" gasped Ashe.

"She was a bit frightened by something," said Creel carelessly. "She'll be all right in another moment."

And as he reached the hall of the house, carrying his burden, she stirred and opened her eyes.

"Ned!" she murmured. "Aye, my dear," he answered. "Are we alive—or dead?"

"Does it matter?" said Creel.

CHAPTER XXIII

ACTION

THAT NIGHT FOUR good men and true sat about a table at Windon Manor. They were John Rincon, little, red, withered, with his tremendous bass voice; Lawrence Payson, big, and pink of face; Robert Lorrimer, with his poet's face, and his fluff of white hair; and Matthew Kingston, broad, silent, and when he spoke it was in a ridiculously thin, small voice. They had been laying plans which, if known, would have forever disrupted the peace of certain reliable and conservative corporations. In a pause of their deeper conversation John Rincon boomed in his vast voice:

"What's the latest bulletin about Anne?"

"She's better," said Lorrimer. "Much better, but still her nerves are on edge."

"What happened to her?" pursued Rincon.

"The devil knows—not I! I sat by her bed for a while this afternoon. She would not talk. And every time I mentioned an automobile the life went out of her face and her eyes." He was silent, frowning.

"Something that Ormonde did," nodded Payson, and he also frowned. "What the devil is in that man?"

"Ask the devil," reiterated Lorrimer. "How should *I* know? Whatever it was that he did, Anne is a nervous wreck. Doctor says she's had some shock. If she doesn't get on her feet in a day or two, I'll go to Ormonde myself and—"

"And what?" cut in Kingston in that sharp tenor; and he stared blankly at Lorrimer.

"I don't know," grumbled the other. "He's a hard man to deal with, but he's got to understand that it's hands off as far as Anne is concerned."

Matthew Kingston smiled unpleasantly.

"He raved about like a wild man this morning," said Payson, "calling for action, action, action! What the deuce did he mean? Can't he get enough action with us? What became of him? I haven't seen him since then."

"He went off with old Garry Barton," said Lorrimer, "still talking about action, and Garry promised that he'd lead him to some game. I don't know what it is, but some deviltry, no doubt. You know Garry's long suit."

"A nervy old hound," nodded Rincon. "At his years you'd think a man would have more common sense. He'll wind up with a trip up the river one of these days."

"Speaking of years and caution," smiled big Lawrence Payson, "you might look at yourself, John."

And John Rincon grinned appreciation of this subtle compliment.

"But what's wrong with the chief? What's up with Ashe?" asked Payson. "He should be here to-night. We need him to work out some of the fine details. No head like Ashe's for the delicate things."

"He's sulking in his room," said Lorrimer, "Hasn't showed his face to a soul except that black-faced pagan of his, that murdering scoundrel of an Afghan. There is a dark streak in Ashe, boys, as we all know, and Ormonde doesn't serve to cheer him up a great deal. I tell you"—and here he lowered his voice to a significant murmur—"there may be a story to tell before many days go by, and you can mark my word for that."

"True!" boomed Rincon. "There was plain murder in his eyes when Ormonde carried Anne into the house. He was close by when she first opened her eyes. Did you hear what she said?"

"No."

"I did, and so did Ashe. She looked up to Ormonde and quavered 'Ned!' and then 'Are we alive—or dead?' And that demon answered: 'Does it matter?' Gad, I've never seen the mate to the look that came in Ashe's face when he heard that bit of dialogue."

"He'd better pocket his gloom," said Lorrimer dryly, "because as far as Anne is concerned, he's done. Whatever Ormonde did to Anne this morning, it was nothing that made her hate him. When I sat by her I talked of a good many things, and her face was as blank as the face of a white French doll until I hit on the name of Ormonde. And then you should have watched the flush go up to her throat. Poor Anne, she's mad about him."

"Why 'poor' Anne?" queried Rincon.

"John, would you have a daughter of yours married to that hard-hearted fiend? Consider this morning. He brought her back a wreck, takes her to her room, and then off to Manhattan with Garry without ever a thought as to whether she's alive or dead."

"Don't be too hard on him," cut in Payson. "He's done enough to prove what he thinks of her."

"Do you think so? I tell you, Lawrie, it was the adventure that drew him to her, and not the girl, bless her! I thought he was tame enough when he first came, but now he's thrown away the reins and there'll be the devil to pay before long."

"There's still work here on the table," broke in the practical mind of Kingston. "Let's get back to it. After they've cleared the rubbish away—what next?"

And they were instantly in the heart of the problem, talking with low voices, as if even in Windon Manor the very walls had ears that might shout their secrets to the world at large. They were interrupted, first by loud voices in the hall, then by a sharp knocking at the door, and finally by the apparition of Garry Barton in their midst.

He wore a cap pulled far down over his eyes and a gray

overcoat with the collar turned up so high that it served to mask the lower part of his face. From the shadow of his visor his eyes gleamed out with alarming brightness. It needed only one glance to tell them that a very frightened old man stood before them.

"The meeting is adjourned," boomed John Rincon, and at the sound of his voice Garry shrank and flashed a glance over his shoulder at the door. "We've got new business on our hands. Out with it, Garry! What's up?"

But Garry Barton was at a loss for adequate expression. He stood close against the wall, shifting from foot to foot and letting his eyes dart furtively from face to face around the table.

"It ain't my fault," he said at last. "Honest to God, it ain't my fault! No matter what you hear, it ain't my fault!"

"It's ten minutes to one," said Matthew Kingston, in that bloodless voice of his, and he laid his watch on the table. "You've got ten minutes to tell your story and put yourself straight, no matter what you've done. Quick!"

And he leaned back to listen.

Garry Barton took off his cap and instantly replaced it, as if the light hurt his eyes. Then he slipped out of his overcoat, which apparently oppressed him with its weight. He revealed a stocky, powerful figure, still agile in spite of his years. His clothes were in tatters, one sleeve almost torn off at the shoulder, a pocket hanging by a shred, rips and tears everywhere, and a dozen vast smears of mud.

Wherever Garry Barton had gone, he had rolled on the ground more than once before he had arrived at his destination. Now he moistened his lips and prepared to speak, and all the while the ominous eyes of the four were fixed upon him without a word.

"You know me," he said at last. "I ain't no moll-buzzer; I ain't no cheap bindle-stiff. I'm blowed-in-the-glass, I am. If things went wrong to-day, it ain't my fault. Say, did I ever ball up the deal before? Did I ever wave a red flag for the dicks to see? Did I ever get trailed to the joint? I'm askin' you, did I?"

And he made a mute gesture of appeal with two grimy palms.

"No," he answered himself. "If I crack a box, I crack it no louder than the poppin' of a toy balloon—that's what old Garry Barton does. Ain't I known for it from coast to coast? Ain't I got my record? Sure I got it!" he agreed with himself. "And now along comes this Ormonde with a rep like a quart of soup and uses it to blow the top off the can and spill my beans! Ain't it hell?"

He made another gesture of misery beyond speech.

"This was the way of it. This toff, he comes to me this mornin', and he says, 'Garry, you got a name for action,' says he, 'and that's what I'm looking for. I want you to lead me where I'll have some fun. Can you do it?'

" 'Sure!' I says. 'A quiet day is a day wasted with me.'

"So we hops a bus and beats it for the big noise. On the way I drops him the straight dope on a nice little deal I got framed. Before I get halfway through talkin' this bird croaks:

" 'I'm not lookin' for a plant. I'm out for excitement. Competition is the thing, Garry. What's the use of lifting the coin for the sake of the coin? Action, Garry—action is what I want.'

"That's the spiel he hands me. I give him the once-over to see if he's kidding me, maybe, but all I gets is the glassy eye. You know? Can't get by that front of his. So I takes him at his word, and plays the fall guy to his Steve Brodie.

"Well, we hit the big town, and this bird says he'd find action somewhere. And as he says it we passes the Northern Reserve Bank. You know the kind of a dump that is—ten feet of tool proof stuff around every dollar and guns scattered from the front door to the fare-thee-well.

"So I says, sort of kidding him: 'There is a joint you can find action in.' And I batted an eye at him.

"But this Ormonde, he don't kid worth a damn. He allowed he'd take a crack at the green-boys. Of course I doped it that he was running a bluff and trying to back me down, so I stuck right with him.

"What did he do? Damn me if I can believe it even after I seen it! He walks straight up to the cashier's window with a whole flock of dicks within ten yards of him, shoves a rod under the bird's nose, and calls for kale—some pocket money, he calls it.

"I begins to sidestep to the door and got my gat ready. I figured that he was crazy, but I wasn't going to go cold on a pal even if he was a nut. I kept an eye out. Mind you, not more'n five people in the dump seen what was happenin'. Mostly it looked just like a guy leaning at the cashier's window talkin' friendly to him. And not a single dick in the gang got wise. The people that did pipe him off was froze in their tracks. A gun don't warm nobody's blood in particular, anyway.

"Then I seen the cashier shove a stack of green-boys out. That cashier was sure a sick-lookin' guy. And this bird Ormonde starts shovin' it into his pockets, sort of careless, as if it was the queer. And then he hollers to me: 'Come on over, Garry, and help yourself!'

"My God, could you beat that? Of course that let me in on the game just as much as if I'd held the rod on the cashier myself. By that time people was waking up, and I seen a couple of the dicks circulating our way. I jumps for Ormonde, grabs one handful of the green stuff, and starts him for the exit.

"We no sooner started than there was hell to pay. People started running from every direction. I seen a dozen guns in the air, but nobody had the guts to shoot in that mess. Ten chances out of eleven he'd have winged the wrong guy.

"So we busted out the door, and hopped a car, and Ormonde started driving us down the street.

"Drove like he was drunk, take it from me. Made a track like a snake dancing. Expert on driving? Well, I got a hunch that maybe he was driving that way just to throw a scare into me, and he done it, all right. He wiggled that car through Fifth

Avenue traffic like a dog weavin' through high grass. I just closed my eyes and hung on and prayed for the finish.

"All hell was breaking loose behind us now. We ducked across town and then we ducked back again—and finally Ormonde stalled the machine at a crossing. Yep, he stalled it, and jumped out of it, still laughing, and slaps me on the shoulder and says: 'This *is* life, Garry!'

"Can you beat that? You can't! And about twenty dicks and bulls coming for us about then! I couldn't make it out. I kept thinkin' about Ormonde and what I'd heard of him bein' smooth as silk and quieter than a snake slipping over a polished floor. And: then I looked at us stalled in the middle of the big noise!

"What did we do? What could we do? We ran like hell and flagged it into a big classy store—women's stuff—and skidded through the first floor, knocking down models and tearing chunks of cloth off the tables and the girls yelling their heads off. A circus? It was!

"But too much noise for me. I like quiet work myself. I mostly prefer the dark. And when we come out of that place the back way I doped it that I'd better tell Ormonde a fond farewell. He was too fast for me. So when we got into the clear again I ducked the nut and let Ormonde flag it wherever he wanted to. But that wasn't all.

"They had a red-hot trail on both of us. I seen part of 'em beat it after Ormonde, but the rest of them stuck on my heels. And now—here I am, but look at me! Do I look like Garry Barton that always got away with his game clean and quiet and hurt nobody's feelings except the boxes I busted? Do I look like him? No, I don't. And did I ever leave a trail before that run all over New York and then come back straight and plain to the hangout?"

Here the four great men at the table showed manifest signs of emotion.

"You fool! You infernal, bungling fool!" thundered little John

Rincon. "Do you mean to stand there and tell me that you left a plain trail to Windon Manor?"

"John," pleaded the cracksman, "I didn't leave it no plainer than I had to. Maybe they got the dope on where I went and maybe they haven't. I dunno. I done my best."

"Of course you did," broke in Lawrence Payson, "but it's the devil! If it hadn't been for Ormonde—"

"Damn his eyes!" burst out Garry uncontrollably.

"But where's Ormonde now?" asked Rincon.

"Probably in jail," suggested the sharp treble of Matthew Kingston.

"Let him rot there, then," thundered Rincon. "Is that what he calls action? Tearing through Manhattan in broad daylight swinging a gun with a crowd chasing him for twelve hours? Is that action? And then come home in rags and tatters with his tongue hanging out like a dog gone mad for drink, probably? I tell you"—and here he smashed his fist down upon the table— "our friend Ormonde may have his overseas reputation, but he'll have to learn that while he belongs in our society he shall not imperil us with his childish and asinine dare-deviltry! Am I right?"

"You are," agreed a chorus.

There was a knock at the door, which was almost immediately set ajar.

"I'm coming in," said the voice, "if this isn't private talk."

And, as the door swung open, they beheld Andrew Creel standing before them. As one man they rose to their feet.

CHAPTER XXIV

SPEAKING OF FOXES

HE WAS DRESSED in faultless evening clothes that fitted him like a glove. His high silk hat was pushed carelessly far back on his head; under one arm was a long package; and he employed himself, as he entered, in drawing off a pair of white gloves as fresh and unstained as if they had been first put on not five minutes before.

"Good evening," said Creel, and he nodded about the group. Then to Barton: "Sorry you left me so early. The fun started later on for me."

Garry Barton, his eyes popping, fell limply into a chair and continued to stare. Creel finished taking off his gloves, stuffed them into a pocket, tossed his hat onto a chair, and sitting down on another he began to undo the long package.

"Are any of you particularly interested in roses?" he inquired politely.

One by one they sat down heavily, their eyes upon him as if hypnotized by his presence.

"I thought that Anne might enjoy them," he went on, "and really they are fine specimens," he continued as he finished unwrapping the box, apparently quite oblivious of the dead silence which had surrounded him since he entered the room.

Here he raised up a dozen roses—long, dull yellow buds on prodigious stems.

"Look at them!" murmured Creel, rapt in his enjoyment of them. "Imagine them in that tall green vase in Anne's room.

133

Imagine them with a wind touching them a bit and waving them, eh? And when they open up, think of the wealth of perfume! They are so bright—see!—they will be almost as lovely in shadow as in the sun. When I saw them first they looked to me like bits of sunshine folded up. I swear they did!"

It was little John Rincon who was first able to speak.

"Mr. Ormonde," he said heavily, "what have you been doing, in the name of God!" Creel stared at his questioner. "In the name of God?" he replied with an irritating brightness. "I've been doing nothing in His name, my dear Mr. Rincon!" And he added as the little man swallowed hard: "What would you have me do? As a matter of fact, I'm just back from a delightful outing—thoroughly enjoying myself for the first time since I left good old England."

He continued rather argumentatively: "Do you know this is really quite a place—this New York. Much more to it than I expected!"

He went on more calmly, leaning back in his chair and half closing his eyes in pleasant, lazy reminiscence.

"Quite a run they gave us. Very rough about it, too. One fellow clipped my hair—see!—with a bullet; and there are a brace or two of holes in the overcoat I was wearing at the time. However, no good thing can last forever. The chase ended and there I was with a roll of greenbacks in every pocket and nothing to do. Distressing, positively!"

He turned to Garry.

"I thought of you, then, Mr. Barton. I really needed some one to step about with and one who might show me the town. However—"

"Mr. Ormonde!" burst out Rincon in his terrific voice.

But Matthew Kingston raised a stubby hand for silence.

"We will listen," he said. "Perhaps Mr. Ormonde will tell us something more about his—party."

Creel surveyed them kindly and yet critically.

"You look at me in the oddest manner," he said carelessly. "I wonder if something has gone wrong here, eh? Well, if you want to hear about my party I'm glad to pleasure you. It really amounts to nothing. Garry and I dropped over to the city this morning, you know, and found ourselves distressingly short of funds, so we dropped in at a bank and borrowed a bit of money. They seemed to regret letting us have it and made a terrible uproar later on, but we went away and paid no more attention to them."

"My God!" broke out Garry Barton in a voice choked and hoarse with unutterable emotion, and he made his familiar gesture of despair to the others.

"D'you hear this? Can you believe it? No, you can't!"

"I don't quite follow you," said Creel, and he surveyed Barton with a calm disapproval, "you seem wrought up about something or other. I fear you have a too highly cultivated imagination, Garry; but you may do in time."

And so saying, by a turn of his shoulder he shut Garry Barton out into the thickest darkness of oblivion.

"I was telling you," he pursued, "that they gave us quite a lively time, and Garry was so hurried that he lost me in the shuffle and, as I have said, I wound up quite alone. However, as they say in the books, a really young man is never down-hearted.

"It required some hunting about, but I finally had a very enjoyable time—dropped in on a little party for tea, borrowed these clothes from a man who assured me that he would never forget me—nice of him, wasn't it?—and then spent the evening at a ball. Wonderful place, wonderful floor, wonderful music, wonderful girls—God bless them! I danced until I was tired out—and here I am ready for bed—so good night to you!"

He rose and sauntered idly toward the door.

"Mr. Ormonde!" shouted little John Rincon, springing to his feet.

"Well?" queried the other from the door.

"Do you realize, sir," thundered Rincon, "that your conduct to-day has been outrageous and such as no self-respecting—"

He stopped an instant.

"Very entertaining," murmured Creel. "Fire away, old fellow!"

"Entertaining?" roared Rincon.

"Hush up!" said Lawrence Payson sharply to little John. "You're following the wrong line entirely, aren't you? Let me put it to you in simple words, Ormonde, if you please. You'll have to bear with me if I seem to be a bit hard on you at times, eh?"

"My dear Lawrie," said Creel, "go quite as far as you like."

"Thanks. Well, that, in the first place, of course you know that we understand and admit your greatness in your specialties and in your own ways. At the same time, Ormonde, it seems to us that our society will be on the brink of exposure to broad daylight if you have another one of these—er—parties. You see?"

"Damned if I do," smiled Creel cheerfully.

"Listen!" argued Payson, keeping his patience by a serious effort. "Don't you really see that if you cavort about Manhattan and the vicinity, raising the devil wherever you go, bursting into banks in broad daylight and then trotting about the streets of New York with most of the police force pot-shotting at you— don't you see," cried Payson with rising violence, "that in about a day or two a few hundred officers will have traced you home to Windon Manor? Good God, Ormonde, don't you see?"

"I admire a strong imagination most awfully," replied Creel, "but you really carry things to extremes. I assure you that there were not more than a hundred officers after me at any one moment to-day. That's honest!"

"Really?" said Payson dryly. "How absurdly dull it must have been for you!"

"But, seriously, Payson," went on Creel, "you mustn't let the police bother you."

"Mustn't I?" snorted Payson, now nearly at the end of his

endurance. "I tell you, Ormonde, I know very little about the English forces of the law, but in America crime is hunted with bloodhound and microscope. A man can't afford to be incautious *once*. There are men in that New York force who have an actual nose for crime. I veritably believe that they can *sense* the wrongs a man has been guilty of. Watch your step, sir. You've pushed us to the edge of a cliff by your—your boyish performance of to-day. Good heavens, the manor may at this instant be surrounded by uniformed men!"

And saying this, he sprang to his feet and pointed a wild arm at the windows. The others cried out with one voice, but Creel shrugged his shoulders and then allowed his amused smile to travel idly from face to face.

"I should be angry with you, Payson," he said at length, "if I didn't see the point in the joke. What reason on earth is there that you and the rest should stay about in such a stupid place as Windon Manor? Why are you afraid that I'm going to lead the police here? And why should you care?"

The rest of the men could not answer. Creel half turned, and in this position he fired his parting shot:

"You fellows can work your plants, as you call them, in stupid security. And then you may drag home your spoils to Windon Manor. For my part, I am not a fox, and I don't live in a hole."

CHAPTER XXV

BURNED FINGERS

HE HAD NO sooner closed the door behind him than the men broke into a clamor of exclamations. John Rincon was for confining the great Ormonde closely until he would solemnly promise to conduct himself in a manner more acceptable to such a conservative portion of the underworld as the inhabitants of Windon Manor.

It was remarked, however, that one cannot clip the wings of an eagle as one can with a hen. And finally Payson voiced the general sentiment when he said: "We have picked a burning coal out of the fire; unless I'm greatly mistaken we'll have our fingers well singed for it."

It was decided to keep a close eye upon the great Ormonde, and whenever he left Windon Manor send one or two reliable men along to keep him from rash acts. But it was not an easy thing to keep an eye on the man. The very next day he rose at noon, slipped away unobserved, and for three days nothing more was seen of him. Nothing was seen, but a great deal was heard.

The region around Windon Manor was filled with great country estates—many acres of trees and flowers and lawns around huge mansions. It was in this near-by field that the terrible Edward Ormonde chose to work.

First the safe in the bank of the neighboring town was blown up—not carefully "souped" and the door knocked off, but such a charge was used that the little building was half wrecked. The spoils of this robbery were not great, but the scandal was immense.

Special detectives in numbers were employed to ferret out the trail of the robber, and Windon Manor quaked to its deepest foundations. Then, one by one, there followed an appalling series of house robberies. After the affair of the bank each house-holder took care to guard his property, but no guards could avail against this spoiler. He was everywhere at once, and where he appeared he left ruin behind him.

A panic seized on the countryside. A house-to-house search for some trace of the spoils was instituted, and Windon Manor itself did not escape surveillance. The society sent out its own emissaries to find Ormonde and bring him back to the manor and his senses, but he could not be found. It was like trailing a bird of passage. Not till the end of the third day was a gay whistling heard from the garden, and then Creel appeared in the garb of a laboring man with a rough blue flannel shirt and heavy shoes.

The heads of the society gathered at once in secret consultation. Ashe himself supervised the proceedings. He said to the four compatriots who sat around the council table:

"Ormonde is back. He is in his room at present. I have established a guard from which he cannot escape, and he will be forcibly detained in Windon Manor at your pleasure. Now let's get down to business and find out what can be done with him."

But no one spoke.

"For my part," said Ashe quietly, "I see no reason why we shouldn't keep him in close confinement until he returns to his senses. Any argument against that?"

"A very good one," replied Robert Lorrimer. "You know that there was a meeting of householders yesterday?"

"Well?"

"For some mysterious reason no one from Windon Manor was asked to attend the meeting."

A grunt from Matthew Kingston.

"So I sent Phil Blackburn to find out what happened. Phil can get into any place in the world where there's a crack in the wall. And he got to this meeting. Well, sirs, that was a very secret and a very angry assemblage, according to Phil. Almost every man in the room had suffered from the crazy plundering of Ormonde, and they had red in their eyes. They wanted blood.

"The temporary chairman made a little talk first, telling them they already knew in general why they had been called together—to find some remedy for the outbreak of crimes in that vicinity. Then he went on to describe the crimes in particular, from the blowing of the safe to the theft of Mrs. Mitchell's brooch. The longer he talked, the madder they became. Before he ended they were growling like dogs. And when he suggested that they form a vigilance committee they positively cheered him."

Even the red face of John Rincon grew pale at that. There is a certain thoroughness and dispatch about vigilance committees that the criminal world likes less than anything in the world.

Lorrimer continued:

"The chairman went on to state that in the room there were representatives of all the notable estates of the countryside with the exception of Windon Manor. He made a little pause there, and then he told them that there was a particular reason for the exception. He gave the reason, and it was not a flattering one.

"My very good friends, they have begun to suspect. Nothing definite as yet, but the suspicion is there; and I would not be at all surprised if that same vigilance committee called on us one of these nights—armed to the teeth and ready for action. There was a murder in the village the other night, and that is blamed on the man who committed the robberies; and somehow or other there is a whisper abroad that that man is connected with Windon Manor. Now, what are we going to do about it?"

"Just this," bellowed John Rincon, pounding the table. "We're going to kick the great Ormonde out of the society. Let him go and take Anne with him."

"That," cut in Ashe, changing color, "is impossible. In the first place, after the services of Ormonde, how could we possibly force him away from us? How could we possibly undo the oaths of fraternity which we have sworn to him?"

"To hell with oaths!" cried Rincon. "Are we all to hang because of one or two miserable oaths? We've got to get rid of this fellow!"

"Rincon," said Ashe—and there was a note almost of pleading in his voice—"stand steady for a little while longer. I give you my word there will be a change in Ormonde. You will hardly recognize him for the same man! I am confident of it."

"Your confidence doesn't budge me," broke in Payson. "I'll tell you frankly, Jimmy, where Anne is concerned you aren't yourself!"

And he faced more or less steadily the murder in the eyes of Ashe.

"Let's bring Anne in and talk with her. She ought to have some idea of what can be done with him," said Matthew Kingston.

The eyes of Ashe wavered and glanced sharply from face to face. He would not acknowledge defeat, but he felt that he was at the end of his rope.

CHAPTER XXVI

THE PASSING OF ORMONDE

THE WHISTLING OF Creel continued while he sat at ease in his room, with his hands locked behind his head and his eyes upon the ceiling, dreaming over the events of the last three days. But by degrees his eyes grew vacant, the whistling fell away, and then his glance centered on something—a spider, perhaps, crawling across the ceiling, or some particular thing out of the host that crowded his memory.

It could hardly have been pleasant, for the gay content faded from his eyes and lines of concern sprang out around his eyes and his mouth. Something very odd was happening in him. He felt as if a light that had been burning within him was burning out—burning low. A certain weariness, ennui, filled him. He rose and began to pace up and down the room. His very step was different. It was not the elastic stride which could fall so noiselessly on the flimsiest of floors. It was a comparatively heavy, inert step.

"I'm tired," thought Creel. But he added, immediately and aloud: "I am Andrew Creel. Ormonde is dead again."

With that he confronted himself in the mirror, and it seemed to him as if he had indeed changed greatly in the passing of the last seconds. His eyes were duller, the lines of his mouth less firm; even his chin did not thrust out with quite the same crispness of outline. Yes, he was once more Andrew Creel.

And now, with a rush of terrifying force, he remembered the crimes of the last days. He had thought at the time that he was merely playing a game—stealing and smashing laws merely to make the society, in the end, throw up its hands and bid him be gone forever from the precincts of Windon Manor. And then he would say: "If Anne goes with me—"

But now he saw clearly that this thinking had been the merest subterfuge. Crime for crime's sake had fascinated him. He had been a thief; he might be a thief again at any moment, if the wild spirit of Edward Ormonde swept once more upon him in the storm wind or in the hush of the night. His first impulse, naturally enough, was to cover the steps of his crimes. He dragged out a valise, and out of it produced a whole armful of plunder.

There was everything in that bag. It was half full of paper money; but the money was only one item. There was jewelry, also, of every description; and there were two or three articles of gold plate from the Cavendish house. Creel stared at the array of plunder, and felt his forehead go cold. Suppose the door of his room were to be swung open—

He rushed to it and locked and double-locked it. Then he sank into a chair, buried his forehead in his hands, and tried to think. He could not even remember the addresses of some of the houses he had pillaged. Then how could he make restitution? Very easily. He would send the entire package to the police and let them restore it to the original possessors. He swept the loot back again into the valise and deposited it once more in a closet.

And still an alarm grew in him like a spreading fire, or like the steadily increasing silence of night. He saw perfectly clearly that it was mere folly now to stay at Windon Manor. His scheme of bluff had failed. There had been no movement to send him from the manor. And as for Anne, Ormonde—the spirit of Ormonde—alone could woo her.

Fool, fool, fool! Why had he not spent all these four days of strength with her, tying her to him with chains of steel? But now it was hopeless.

He would go down to the garden and walk there, thinking

out some means of escape. He opened the door of his room, but as he did so, a man appeared out of nothingness and motioned him back to his apartment.

"Orders," said this new fellow whom he had never before seen about the manor.

"You stay in your room; I stay here and *see* that you stay. Take it easy and everything is O.K. But start a fuss and I go the limit. See?"

Creel slipped back into his room without a word.

This, then, was the end. He knew it not so much because they had placed the guard over him as because he felt that there was little in his make-up now which needed guarding. All the spirit of the destroyer was gone. There remained only the innocuous calm of Andrew Creel.

It grew upon and gathered around him like a fog. But not long; for he had hardly sunk again into the chair when there was a knock at the door. He opened it and found Anne Berwick standing in the hall.

She was dressed in a dull yellow dress with pastel shades brightening it toward rose and dimming it toward green here and there; she stood very still, smiling at him in such a way that her eyes seemed looking past him. She was quite pale, and with the darkness behind her she looked like a portrait of a beauty rather than living beauty itself.

When she had come into the room and the light fell full upon her he saw that she was almost colorless; and there was a peculiar dullness about her eyes, compared with the keen sparkle which had always lived in the eyes of Anne Berwick in the days before.

"They sent me to you," she said quietly. "Otherwise, I should not have come."

The words might have carried a connotation of scorn, but there was no scorn in the sound of her voice.

"I know you despise me, Ned, since I showed the white feather the other morning. Well, I despise myself. But that has nothing to do with it. I've been sent up to do a thing tactfully. I can't. I'll simply repeat the gist of the message. "You've been so—active—Ned, that you've started the hornets buzzing and Ashe and the rest are afraid that suspicion has been drawn toward Windon Manor.

"In a word they want you to cut away from the society, throw up the oaths that bind you to it, and it to you, and cut away—in any direction you choose. That's all. What answer shall I take them? Are you willing to give up your bad bargain so easily?"

It was here; it was his release! And yet his heart did not leap. For perhaps he was looking his last on Anne Berwick at this moment.

"And you, Anne?" he asked dully.

She smiled in a strange manner once more. There was no mirth in it.

The head of Creel fell.

"I will not hold you to our bargain. You are free except for your own will, Anne."

She shook her head, murmuring: "I knew it would be this way. I could read it in the sound of your voice, Ned."

A shadow of Ormonde's impudence stiffened him. He stepped close to her.

"Anne," he demanded, "what do you mean? Will you tell me that you care for me—the least in the world?"

"Oh," she said, "don't you see?"

And if he had not known that she was Anne Berwick he would have thought that there were tears in her eyes. His arms went out to her, circled her slowly; she pushed them away.

"Wait!" she pleaded hurriedly, "Ned, you mustn't say what you are about to say. I'm going to be utterly frank with you. I'm not the Anne Berwick you first met. I've no more courage—no more decision—no more sharpness of mind. Ned, it all went out of me on that terrible and wonderful ride.

"I don't know what did it. But I saw you for the first time, and it was like breathing fire. I was afraid; I'm still afraid of you. I saw how much stronger you are than I have ever been, and seeing that I've come to dread all the world of adventure and danger you live in. Ned, if you were to take me with you it would be one long torture. Once I could have shared your life; now I would simply be a shivering outsider, frightened every moment you were out of my sight. Do you understand? Do you see what a weak, miserable creature I've become?"

He broke into a laughter of almost hysterical violence and at the end he caught her close to him.

"Anne," he murmured at her ear, "don't you see that for you I'd give it all up—in a moment?"

But she whispered sadly:

"How—in an impulse—you think so. But what of the years to come? What when the old, fierce urge comes back to you?"

"Even then," he answered, "you would be stronger—our love would be stronger, Anne. Will you go with me?"

"To the end of the world."

"And we'll start a clean life, a new life, Anne?"

"With all my heart!"

"And when the old urge comes back in me I'll trust in you to fight it away," he said, drawing her closer.

"Oh, my dear," she said, "you've no idea how hard I shall try!"

And her arms tightened around him.

AUTHOR'S NOTE

MANY A WEIRD day and many a sharp moment lay before Andrew Creel after the time when he stood with Anne Berwick in his arms; but the crises which followed he had to meet with the single force of Creel and not with the mysterious addition of Edward Ormonde's force.

Creel himself is firmly convinced that during those grim days at Windon Manor another personality—the soul of the famous dead criminal—had taken possession of him. But there is another explanation—less mysterious, almost too simple.

There are two souls in every man, and two selves. The one self is that which other men see; the self which walks the streets and labors and earns bread money and sweats and groans and struggles under burdens; and succumbs to pressure; and cries for mercy; and creeps into a grave at last unknown and un-noticed.

There is another self. It is more vividly present in the child; a self which accomplishes great deeds with a consummate ease, which laughs at fear, which knows neither weariness nor self-doubt, which lives mightily in every day and sleeps every night a dreamless sleep.

That secondary self too commonly dies when childhood ends or it lives on only to give color to those dreary nightmares—the day dreams of middle-age; but there are moments, impulses, when that submerged self rises and takes us by the throat. It is the impulse which makes the mountaineer yearn to throw himself from the height, perhaps; aye, and it may be the impulse which gives the poet his impetus, and the musician his dream, and lets the sculptor see the delicate grace which lies concealed beneath the rugged outlines of the block of stone.

It is the impulse, perhaps, which makes every one of us now and again wish to burst the bonds of convention and necessity and live for one moment, one hour, one day, a life of freedom, a life of intoxicating liberty.

His family, his work, the familiar pictures on his wall, are at times the most damnable of burdens. They are part of the sham figure which the world accepts as the whole truth about the man. But deeply within he knows that it is *not* the full truth. There is inside him a strong, free, beautiful, and a terrible spirit. And that spirit springs up into life now and again. It burns him with a flame, and like a flame it terrifies him. The wild desire to be that hidden self, to realize that true personality in action for a moment becomes the one worth while thing in life. The next moment the passion dies away. The man is frightened by the strangeness. He shrinks back to his prison cell and strokes the familiar walls of stone.

Yet time and again the most common of us have a single instant's liberation. Perhaps it comes with that burst of light which men term love—that incredible thing which, if it be real, exhausts itself in a glance. Perhaps that freedom and the existence of that buried self is taught us through the pain of a great grief. But whether it be joy or sorrow that teaches us the existence of the hidden self it is like a flame, and burns itself away. Aye, and if it persists, it may consume the other self also.

Andrew Creel escaped the penalty. But it was not, as he supposes fondly to this day, the personality of Edward Ormonde which possessed him; it was his own inner self which took possession of him. Like Prometheus, he stole the fire of heaven. But, unlike Prometheus, he was spared from the vulture.

ABOUT THE AUTHOR

MAX BRAND IS a Californian who saw the West first in the central valley of the State, where the Coast Range ran low on one side and the Sierra Nevadas on clear days were green and brown over the foothills, and blue or glass-white above. He learned something of cattle and cattlemen among the great grasslands of the foothills, but he never was so deep in that Old West which is a golden legend to-day, as when he spent a few weeks with two old trappers near the Diablo Mountains, close to El Paso, in Texas.

Nick and Alec had fought Indians, ridden range, prospected for gold, made fortunes for others, and had never been able to spend all the wealth that had poured in upon their minds. Some of the glory of mountains and desert remained with them as a perpetual heritage. Nick, at seventy-eight, had a body bent and twisted by age; Alec at eighty was straight as a stick, with no visible sign of the passage of time about him. But Alec was apt to blame his inability to read upon a defect of his eyes.

They quarreled constantly. To Max Brand, Nick reported that Alec was just a touchy old idiot—who could not even read! And what is a man capable of when he cannot read print? Alec, with equal fervor, reported that poor Nick was not to be blamed for weakness of temper and mind, for, said Alec, when a man's body is bent his brain is sure to sag also! But in spite of their wrangling, the two loved one another with a perfect devotion. And the long tales which they told in the evenings, making

sixty years of Western history breathe
and repainting mountains and deserts,
have never been out of the mind of
Max Brand. Nothing is more vivid to
him than the memory of the little
shanty near the "tank," the small
stretchers on which the skins of coyotes
and bobcats were drying, and the
wrangling voices of old Nick and Alec.

Max Brand

Max Brand has been a traveler for
a great many years, from the Pacific
Islands to the deserts of northern Africa, but when he search-
es for stories, he most often goes back to that shanty in Texas,
and the voices of the two old men pour up in his mind. That is
why Western themes generally have come off his typewriter
during the last sixteen years. In fact, he has written more
Western stories than any other author. He is forty years old,
was born on the Coast, spent twenty-three years in California,
and since that time has lived east and west in diverse parts of
the world.

THE ARGOSY LIBRARY ™